I0576243

# COTTONWOOD

*A Novel*

Stacy Dean Campbell

EAST NASHVILLE PRESS

2026

*EASTNASHVILLE PRESS 2026*



ISBN 979-8-9943270-4-3

Published in the United States by

EAST NASHVILLE PRESS

*For Presley, Eva and Ella*

# COTTONWOOD

THE LEATHER STRETCHED and creaked and tore little hair-fine tears along its edge like old stressed tendon pulling away from bone. Two remaining nails long since rusted and near headless grabbed the wood tight and held fast. Dangling limp from the homemade hinge, the screen door swayed in the tepid breeze, its latch clacking against the jamb taunting and teasing the strike plate. Holes so big in its mesh a small bird could fly right through without even touching his feathers on the little rusty barbs that curled and gnarled and stuck out every which way, same as hair does when you burn it. A small bible lay open atop the flaking layers of paint on the porch rail and the pages blew back and forth from Proverbs to Psalms. A fly landed on Proverbs 11:22, rode the bucking page for a moment then flew off through a hole toward the kitchen. It was mid-August. Heat hung. A damp wool blanket rolling in vapors like gas fumes across fields of short brown brush speckled white with cotton.

A black speck pulled a caliche cloud up the sunbaked strip full of ruts and rock that wound back toward the highway before it crooked again and led up to the front yard of the house. A faint buzz grew to a struggling growl as the sedan bounced on to the gravel drive and rocked hard forward and then back again before it slumped into its temporary resting place. The house, wood frame in its construction and perched atop a retaining wall formed from concrete and odd shapes and sizes of smooth, white river rock had begun to settle causing it to sag on its west side. A chalky auburn haze streaked the pockmarked tin of the roof where it bent, waving in curls across the steep pitch. The front easement jutted forward like a huge crooked nose, broken and mended and broken again. The door of the sedan swung open and a gold county sheriff emblem, etched into the onyx lacquer, shot a reflected sunbeam up across the porch before the door swung back shut, snuffing out the bright little glint and leaving the porch again gray and drab and void of anything that shined. He stood beside the car and listened to the eerie silence of the hardscrabble property and wondered to himself why this near uninhabitable house hadn't been torn down years ago.

A worn leather holster hung from a belt cinched around his waist and he unsnapped its strap and left it to lie draped across the hammer of a blued .38 revolver. Unsnapping the pistol had just become what he had called a nervous habit and he appeared more cautious and methodical than scared as he approached the porch. The rotten planks of the steps strained under his weight and he stepped from the bottom up to the top without touching the middle for fear that it would give and snap out from under him. The paper of the little bible rattled in the breeze. He walked to where it lay, closed the cover and moved it down from the rail and placed it on the sill of the front window.

"Hypocrite," he mumbled under his breath, then spat on the dirty glass and rubbed out a clean spot with the heel of his hand, wiped the grime on his pant leg and pushed his face as near to the window as he could without bending the brim of his hat. Dust particles filled the air and floated on the streaks of sun that pushed through the thin slits in the heavy draperies. From the window he could see the front room and back through part of the kitchen. Lamps and lights burned dim and oozed a sickly jaundiced glow out across the walls. A small wooden table sat beside a tweed chair with wounds stitched and restitched, scarring its back and arms. A corked glass bottle sat on the table behind a squatty jar that had the words Kerr SELF-SEALING MASON blown three dimensional on its side. A rank oily liquor puddled shallow in its well.

"Where the hell you at, you crazy bastard?"

He talked to himself as he moved to the edge of the porch and leaned out and looked down the side of the house toward the back yard.

A skinny dog with matted clumps for hair walked around the far side of the porch and squatted her haunches in the dense milkweed that filled an overgrown flowerbed. The scuff of the man's boot startled the dog and she flinched and snarled and barked out at the intruder. The man wheeled about with the revolver half drawn. He eased the pistol back into his holster and plucked a dirt clod from a potted plant that hung next to his head and slung it with the full force of his arm. It disintegrated popping like a firecracker off the edge of the porch, peppering the dog's muzzle. She let out a loud yelp and tucked her tail and ran.

"Damned old bitch dog! You scared the hell outta me!" He waved his arm as he yelled at the scalded dog disappearing back around the side of the house.

He walked back over to the front door and knocked heavy on the screen.

"Walters, you in here? Walters?"

The bottom of the screen door dragged on the porch following a path well-worn to a quarter circle. It was cool when he stepped inside. Stock-still and hollow. A small fan covered in greasy dust sat on the floor pointing toward the bedroom at the end of the hall. As it hummed and oscillated it stirred the smells of stale whiskey and burnt coffee and mixed them with the putrid scent of urine and antiseptics that wafted from the bathroom. Patchwork quilts with pretty floral designs of textured denims and heavy twills hung listless from the bedroom window frames, blocking out the cleansing rays of the afternoon sun.

The man pulled a handkerchief from his hip pocket and mashed the fresh fabric tight to his nose.

"Hey, Guppy, you in here?"

He stood there in the stillness a moment then stepped back out into the thick, muggy air of the West Texas afternoon. The black sedan once again pulling the caliche cloud down the crooked road back toward the highway.

**ESTHER**

SHE INCHED ALONG THE ROAD silhouetted
against the burnt orange sky of morning. It was a long walk
but she had covered half of it by the time the darkness had
been pushed up off the sharp black line of the horizon. She
was not a small woman, but she was a deliberate one and
every step she placed onto the chalk-covered gravel of the
road was careful and soft, almost choreographed into some
fluid motion perfected through familiarity. She wore a
robin's egg blue cotton dress that hung to the middle of her
shin, a thin piece of eyelet crimped around the hem. The
fabric dark and moist in the cracks where her upper arms
pressed into her torso and down the middle of her back
where sweat followed the zipper and disappeared at the

waist-line. The dress blossoming away from her body into the pleated skirt that moved and breathed and swished back and forth about her legs as she walked. She stopped and lifted her right foot and removed her shoe and turned it upside down and bobbled on one leg in a careful attempt to keep the exposed stocking from touching the rough ground while she shook the shoe wildly. Tiny gravels dropping back down onto the road as she hopped about, her right arm extending and waving like an acrobat keeping his balance on a tightrope. She pushed the shoe back onto her foot and continued her course. As she neared the stone walk that led up to the front porch of the big white farmhouse, she pressed the fingers of her right hand together fashioning a makeshift iron and rubbed at the fabric all about herself, licked the fingers and slid them across her scalp securing any stubborn wayward hairs. Three hard knocks on the door announced her arrival.

"Come on in, it's open," Rube yelled at the screen door and Esther quietly stepped into the front room.

"Well good mornin', Esther. I didn't realize that was you. What brings you all the way out here so bright and early?" Rube said as he stepped from the kitchen and saw her standing in the entry.

"Good mornin' to you, Sheriff Whitlock. I just come out this mornin' hopin' I could talk with you about the help you needin'," she rubbed her hands together as she talked,

"PV stays so busy all day long and it's all I can do to keep from goin' outta my ever- lovin' mind since my babies done grown and gone."

Rube wiped at his hands with a dishrag and stepped toward Esther.

"Come on around and sit down," he said.

"Thank you, I b'lieve I will."

"Tell the truth Esther, I hadn't wanted to have to get anybody at all, but 'tween sheriffin' and tryin' to feed those boys every time I turn around it's a wonder I manage to get anything done. How's old PV doin' anyway, heard he got himself another mule." Without realizing it, Rube shook his head as he talked.

"That's right, he sure did. He's got the grand notion all right, he'd scratch up the whole state of Texas if I didn't make him stop to eat supper once in a while."

"Well, Lizbeth just ain't been the same since we lost the baby you know," Rube said as the mood shifted to somber.

"Yessuh, I's sure sorry to hear about that. Must be harder than I know."

"It is, it sure is and I just need someone to help me keep the place up. Maybe stay some evenings with the boys 'til I can get done with work and get home. I had liked to think that we could manage but it's been some time since we had on fresh clothes and Lord knows we ain't gainin' no weight off my cookin'." He laughed and tugged at his belt. "I cain't pay all that much but I sure could use the help and any food that we had left over you could take a supper plate on out to PV, save you havin' to do twice the cookin'."

"Yessuh."

"Well the sooner you could start the better."

Esther straightened her dress and glanced around the room, "Well, it's too hot to just turn around and walk on back home." She smiled and stuck out her hand and Rube took it and shook.

# HOME

APHIDS THICK AND LIME GREEN bit like chiggers when they landed on your skin. June bugs and fat furry moths hung in the screen and darted in at the light every time you held the door open for more than a few seconds at a time. I often wondered if they had known what they were getting into, they might not have been so anxious to fly into our house. The summer that Esther came to work for us I remember feeling the weight of the world pushing down on my shoulders and me pushing back as hard as I could. And I pushed Esther just as far as she would let me push her every chance I got. I remember thinking, before that summer, there really was a whole lot of difference between me and the coloreds. More than just the shade of our skin. I used to think like a lot of the others around here. That dark brown skin just had to have something to do with not washing. Surely that had something to do with it. Then I'd see Esther washing her hands so much that they'd wrinkle. Looking back, I guess that she was the first negro I had ever really been around. Oh, I had seen plenty of them. Fact is I had seen her before, lots of times, just not up close. Seen her walking one time with a black man. I can remember thinking to myself that he was wearing a hat almost just like daddy's. Felt and clean and tipped just a bit to the side. I had no idea that she'd ever be in our house doing all the things mama used to do. She even sewed a pair of pants for me one time when I ripped them on a barbed wire fence. Couldn't even tell that they had been mended at all. I remember changing a lot that summer. Life seemed to get harder after that. The world started to spin faster and faster, the days just flying off into the wind like children on a merry-go- round, trying to hang on until the spinning just slings them off into the grass, some landing soft and full of laughter and some slamming down hard and just sitting down and crying.

Daddy was a farmer and a Mason and more than likely a Klansman with a little bit of land out of Wellington, Texas. If you were to ask him he'd probably tell you that he was only a part-time sheriff, just making ends meet until he could get the 75 acres that butted up to the back of our place. Everybody in town knew it was really the other way around. We all knew that he'd never get those acres. Deep down he knew it too. Elgie always said that I wasn't nothing but a foul-mouthed, hell-bound heathen trying to be just like daddy but I couldn't because I was born with one leg shorter than the other. Elgie was a hypocrite. He said he wanted to be a preacher someday, but get him riled and he'd cuss same as me and daddy. Eloise was out behind the rose bushes in a seventy-five dollar pinewood box that the worms had probably ate through the day after she was put there. She was so full of pus and infection they more than likely gobbled her up inside a week. Mama's head was hollow as Eloise's box. She had made Daddy put Sister out there behind her rose bushes instead of in the graveyard like everybody else. When Mama wasn't in bed, she was in a chair staring out the window. I walked down the hall one day and the door to Mama's room was standing open a piece. I peeked in there and saw her sitting in front of the mirror pulling a small, silver-handled brush through her wavy red hair. The milk-white skin of her arms bled into her white cotton dress. I would have thought that it was long sleeved if it hadn't been for the pattern of small red flowers that wound its way all around the fabric. Her voice was soft and raspy from not talking a lot, I suppose, and I could hear little broken verses of "Tis So Sweet To Trust In Jesus" coming from her lips, which were painted a shade of red much like the little roses. Daddy came around the corner with a cup of coffee in his hand and saw me there in the hallway where I knelt staring into my parents' room.

"What are you doin, Arliss?"

"I was just watchin' mama. She's all dressed and fixed up and she's singin'."

"I know. Ain't that the damnedest thing. She just come in this mornin' and said she might wanna go into town for a bit. Don't that beat all."

"Ya'll gonna go?"

"Yeah, I guess we will. Why don't you go get Elgie and we'll all go. Ain't no sense in ya'll just sittin' around here all day."

Every once in a while Daddy would surprise us like that. Turn and just act flat out nice. Like he didn't have a care in the world. Like everything was the way it had always been. Maybe it was Mama and the thought of her getting better that made him act that way. Although, I had seen her sing and primp before and he would still act rough as a cob. He was hard to see coming. That's why most of the time we just tried to stay out of his way. "Live your life the best you can," that's what Elgie would say when it would sometimes get the best of me. I'd try to ask him why he thought Daddy was the way he was and he'd just tell me that God gives everybody a certain life and that's the life you get so you might as well just make the best of it. Most of the time that's what I did.

I went in and woke up Elgie. He was as surprised as me but he jumped right up and started pulling at his clothes.

By the time Elgie got dressed and we got outside, Daddy was standing on the front porch with a fresh cup of coffee and staring out across the yard. He looked at us with distance in his eyes and we knew what he was gonna say.

"Your mama ain't feelin' so good as it turns out and we ain't goin'. I might just go on anyway. There's some things I need to tend to. Ya'll go on now and do your chores. I'll be back directly." His soft tone had turned stern again and we knew not to ask if we could go along.

I watched as Daddy walked out past the big shiny sedan and crawled onto the seat of his old farm truck and hung his elbow out the window. He saw me standing in the front door behind the screen and he raised his hand to wave. I just edged over a bit and pretended like I didn't see him. The truck bed was empty and though I knew he was probably going to fill it with the heavy burlap sacks of feed that would scratch at his arms and make him itch anyplace that they touched on his skin I still wanted to go. It seemed that more and more, Daddy didn't want me and Elgie to be around him. Even when we were working as hard as we could, it seemed that we were just doing things wrong in his eyes. I pulled the curtain to the side and watched as he pulled away. Elgie walked off towards what he called his "reading tree" and I turned and caught myself walking towards Mama's room. She had always been so easy to talk to. She always knew what to say in times like these. I knew now that she barely even knew who I was. I walked back out on to the front porch and listened as two birds somewhere high and far removed from this place sat and called back and forth. It seemed strange how they could be so close to me and my house and all this sadness and yet be in a whole other world. The way they sang. Happy. Maybe that's the way Mama was. She sat right in the middle of us so far away. I didn't know where her world was most of the time, but I hoped wherever it was that it had something about it that made her happy. Elgie said that it might just be the only place that she could go to get close to Eloise. I knew that if he was right, she'd more than likely stay there. Elgie would say stuff like that sometimes. He'd be standing there all day dreamy looking and then just like that, he'd open his mouth and out it would fall. Maybe God put those things in his mouth. I don't know, I never really questioned it much. I just listened when it happened and tried to appreciate it for what it was.

I stepped back out on to the porch and sat down in Mama's old, cane-backed rocking chair and watched and listened to our farm. It was a pretty place when you just stopped and looked at it. Calm and peaceful when Daddy was gone. He seemed to snag the big, dark, gray blanket that covered our home on the bumper of his truck and drag it off behind him down the road as he went. You could almost see the color soaking back in as he drove away. I noticed things when he was gone. Just how bright green the stalks and leaves get on the corn plants in the garden or how far a grasshopper can fly. Especially if you flick it with your finger. There was a small cluster of purple and white wildflowers growing up in the middle of all the grass and weeds that had long since taken over the little bed that ran along the bottom front of the porch. Mama dug and dug on that bed until it was nothing but soft, rich, dark, brown soil. She let me and Elgie crawl along in front of her and poke our fingers down into it while she followed behind dropping little seeds into the shallow holes, pushing the dirt in on top of them and patting at it with her hand. I watched as a bee landed in the middle of the soft petals and made use of the persistent little wildflowers. I wondered if God would give the honey that they would produce a little sweeter taste as a reward for their effort.

I had been in such a hurry to get outside that I hadn't even noticed her in the kitchen. When I walked back inside there she was, wiping her hands on a towel that she had tucked into a gap between two buttons on the front of her dress. Her smile was warm and sincere, but I didn't want to like her. I didn't really want to like anybody at that particular moment. I guess with me she never really had much of a chance.

"You just got to be Arliss," she said as she patted at the side of her hair.

"I don't got to be but I am. Who might you be?"

"My name is Esther and it's nice to meet you."

"Might I ask what tha hell you doin' here in tha kitchen?"

"Well, at the moment I'd be wipin' this old dirty dish water offa my hands. It's been on 'em so long they startin' to look like a couple of old prunes. Your daddy hired me on just this mornin' to help out around the house. I was just thinkin' I might make some biscuits and gravy. If that's awright with you?"

"You mean you gonna live here?"

Oh she noticed the sarcasm in my voice alright and the shape of her mouth sank from the warm smile to a tight lipped grimace.

"No, I mean I'm gonna work here. If'n you aim to eat here this mornin' then you best go call your brother, who I have not had the pleasure to meet yet, and the two of you get yourselves washed up. I been makin' biscuits and gravy ever since I can remember and it don't take me no time at all." She had her hands on her hips and her head moved slightly from side to side as she talked.

She turned back to her biscuits and continued matter-of-factly cutting out circles in the dough with the lid of a canning jar. That's the way I first remember meeting Esther.

## ROSIE

THE LATCH HAD BEEN STIFF and hard to turn for some time and he cussed it as he jerked it and rammed the door with the meaty part of his shoulder. The door eventually gave and he lunged forward out of the truck, just catching hold of the frame and stopping an embarrassing face-first fall on to the middle of the street. He popped back up next to the truck and slammed the door. The air was thick and he had already sweat through the back of his shirt and partly through the strap on his overalls. The sun was bearing straight down on his head and he could feel the rays as they passed through the tiny holes in his straw hat and sat on his scalp like embers.

"Piece of junk," he said under his breath.

"How you doin' this afternoon, Rube?" Rube turned and saw a small-framed man sitting on a bench on the sidewalk.

"Oh I guess I ain't gonna complain. How you, Newton? Don't know anybody who'd be in the market for a damn fine farm Ford do ya?" Rube grinned as he stepped toward the man and held out his hand.

The man made no effort to remove himself from his perch, but did take the outstretched hand and give it an over exaggerated shake.

"Well I sure as hell don't need another headache with the whole damn town overrun with smart aleck, high-thinkin' niggers. Guess you heard 'bout old PV and his new buckskin jenny? Ain't that the damnedest thing. Ain't that just the damnedest thing, Rube? Where's your sedan at anyhow?"

Newton finished the whole little speech without so much as taking a breath, then turned and spit a four-inch-long stream of brown, grainy liquid out over the curb. The tobacco juice hit the ground with a splash and Rube turned and admired the distance and accuracy of the shot.

"Yeah Newton, I heard about PV's new mule. So has everybody else in this and the three neighborin' counties. His old field ain't nothin' but rock and sand anyhow. The way everybody's goin' on and on about it you'd think that old mule was gonna just plow everybody under."

"It ain't that, Rube. It's just the principal of the thing. Hell, I just think it's embarrassing for people to drive around down here and see that old fool out there scratching around that's all, it's just embarrassing."

Rube didn't say anything more about PV, his mule or Esther or anything else, he just smiled and shook his head. He caught a glimpse of his reflection in the glass that filled the picture window behind Newton's head. CAFE painted in big red letters, chipped and faded in an upside down crescent moon across its center.

"They any pie left this mornin'?"

"Hell I don't know. Darlene's in a mood, I's too scared to ask."

Two little silver bells hanging from a cotton string on the inside of the door clanked and clattered as he straightened his shirt collar and stepped into the room. The smell of coffee drifted on a haze of blue-gray smoke. He breathed deep and patted the bib of his overalls, reassuring himself that he had not forgotten his cigarettes. Once reassured, he walked across the room and took a seat at the counter. The legs on the stool that he chose were uneven from years of disproportionate patrons scooting it in and out from under the bar, and he pushed it back and pulled out the stool next to it, only to find that it too was uneven. As he sat on the stool it rocked back and forth. The illusion nautical; a sailor dining in a galley on a calm evening sea.

Rube took his hat off and sat it on the first stool. He steadied himself by leaning forward and resting his forearms on the ledge in front of him. A woman approached him carrying a thick, eggshell-colored cup on a thick, eggshell-colored saucer. Her hair, bound beneath a flimsy string net broke free from its restraints. The wispy brittle sprigs lunging and whipping in the breeze stirred by a fan that gurgled in the serving window and offered the only frontline defense against the stagnant air that filled the room. She was probably in her early thirties, but smoke and grease mixed with heat, humidity and two small fatherless children had long since taken their toll, giving her the look of a much older woman. Tired. World-worn. She set the cup and the saucer down as if they had jumped on to the counter top. Coffee sloshed from the cup and splashed on to the saucer and then on to the counter before settling back in the cup and she wiped at it with an apron that looked like the hide of a paint mustang, white and stained with several brown patches.

"Apple, peach, cherry and maybe, uh, one or two slices of mince left," the woman said with a smile and turned and walked back in the direction which she had just come. She disappeared through two small doors that swung at her, barely missing her backside as she stepped through them.

"Mince, Darlene," Rube yelled at the doors as he lifted the cup and blew at the hot coffee.

"Gimme just a minute, hun," her voice called back from somewhere behind the wall.

"Take your time."

The slap on his back caused more coffee to slosh from the cup and splash on to the counter. Had the cup been to his mouth, it would have scorched his lips and tongue.

"Damn. I'm sorry, Rube. I didn't even see yer coffee."

"That's quite alright, Virg. It don't seem to be in the cards for me to drink much of this cup anyhow. Pull up a stool, they got uh, apple, peach, b'lieve she said cherry and maybe one more slice of mince left."

"Darlene, bring a slice'a peach if you would," Virgil shouted at the two swinging doors.

There was no answer and Virgil looked at Rube.

"Think she heard me?" he asked.

"I think she heard ya, Virg. Just don't think she likes ya," Rube grinned as he got his first sip from the coffee.

"Aw hell," Virgil said as he looked back at the doors, "I don't think she heard me. Darlene?"

There was still no answer, but Darlene reappeared in front of them holding a piece of mince pie in her left hand, a saucer and a cup of coffee in her right hand and balancing a piece of peach pie on her right forearm. Virgil received the same style delivery of his coffee and she wiped again at the liquid adding another brown patch to the hide. She softly set a neatly cut piece of mince pie down in front of

Rube and slid the other plate across the counter at Virgil. The peach pie was in a blob in the middle of the plate.

"Sorry, Virgil. Tore it up gettin' it outta the pan. Stills tastes good though. Some things is deeper than just looks, ya know." Darlene glared at Virgil and then disappeared again behind the swinging doors.

Rube laughed out loud and shoved a big chunk of the mince pie into his mouth.

"Now what in hell did I do to her?" Virgil asked as he poked at the blob of peach pie on his plate.

"I think it's what you didn't do to her that's got her upset," Rube laughed again at himself and small little crumbs shot from his mouth and ricocheted, unnoticed by him, off the counter as he chewed violently at the warm pie.

"Aw hell," Virgil said looking back at the doors.

"Aw hell," he said again and then scooped a fork full of the pie from his plate and shoveled it into his mouth.

"Say Rube, you heard about PV's new mule?"

Rosie was a knobby-kneed buckskin out of Harmon County, Oklahoma somewhere over by Vinson. She stood about sixteen hands at my best guess and had probably pulled half the plows in West Texas at least two or three hundred miles. She belonged to Otis Ussery. Everybody around here just called him PV. Nobody really knew where that name came from and nobody ever really seemed to care enough to ask. PV fancied himself a farmer with most of his efforts concentrated on sweet potatoes, peanuts and other small crops - his ambitions on cotton like everybody else. He swore off technology saying that hay and feed was still cheaper than gasoline and he could bust a lot more rows on two bellies full of oats and alfalfa than he ever could on a tank full of gas. Talk around was that he gave a hundred and fifty dollars for Rosie. Daddy said one time that he got cheated, "'cause that old mule wasn't fit to feed and only a niggra would've give that for that old bag of bones, buckskin or not." I saw Daddy and PV shake hands one time, and I could have sworn that they were friends the way they talked. Daddy never talked about him the way he talked about his other friends though, and I had to ask Elgie just what a nigger was the first time I heard daddy call a black man that. Whatever they called them, it sure caused a stir when PV showed up with Rosie and hooked that team up to that old, rickety middle-buster and started breaking ground. I don't know that any colored in the history of Wellington had ever been so ambitious as to own two mules. The one that was, just happened to be married to Esther.

Rube finished the last bite of his pie and reached into the pocket on the front of his overalls, pulled out a small leather pouch and laid it out in front of him. He pulled the puckered top of the pouch open and peeled out a small rectangular paper and cupped it into a ditch between his left index finger and his thumb. With his right hand he reached into the bag again, pinched at its contents and rubbed his fingers together so that the small brown strings of moist tobacco crumbled and floated down in a steady flow into the little paper ditch. Once the tobacco was evenly spread, he rolled up the delicate paper, licked it and pushed the neat little tube three fourths of its length into his mouth and propelled it out again until it hung by its tip on the corner of his lip. He picked a wooden match from a box there among the salt and pepper shakers and scratched it under the edge of the counter and held the dancing fire to the work. He slung his hand and the flame jerked and disappeared in a wisp of smoke like a tiny dissipating apparition. Rube breathed a long deep breath and let the smoke billow out of his nostrils like the heavy smoke of damp pine burning and seeping up and out of a cold chimney pipe. He stared at Virgil for a long time before he answered.

"Yeah, I have, and I think I've 'bout damn near heard all I want to hear about that old mule too. Is that all anybody around here has got to talk about?" Rube looked at Virgil and took another long pull off the cigarette.

"Naw, I's also wanderin' if you put old Guppy in the tank the other night?" Virgil slurped at his coffee.

"Naw, I just run eem off from over at the Lodge is all. When I got over there he was standin outside hollerin' like the crazy fool he is, pants clear down around his ankles and pissin' on the side of the building. Some of 'em over there was afraid he was gonna tear up their cars. I went up and told him to holster his tallywhacker and go home and sleep it off or he could come spend the night down at my little motel. He went off justa cussin' me." Rube puffed on the cigarette and squinted as the smoke curled around his eyes and drifted off over his head.

"He sure is one touched old bastard ain't he?" Virgil said as he scraped his fork all around the edge of the plate picking up the last remaining traces of the pie. He put the fork in his mouth and pulled it back out through clinched lips and set it back on the counter, squeaky clean atop his napkin as though it had never been used.

"Oh, he's touched alright. That's for damn sure."

## TWO BIT BARLOW

THE SKY OOZED DEEP PURPLE through that half-dead Loblolly Pine that stood tall and thin and scraggly outside the window of our room. Honeysuckle perfume drifted sweet and soft and I can remember Elgie saying that it always made him think of mama back before she got sick, and me thinking the very same thing. Elgie lay closest to the window 'cause he was older. The night air always felt cool as the sounds of the nightstalkers and the dark-world feeders came to life. A cricket must have lived right out there on the sill, because I'd almost swear I could smell rosin when he started rubbing his legs together.

"Hey, Elgie you awake? Elg, you awake? Elg, wake up!"

"What do you want Arliss," Elgie said trying to sound irritated.

"Ain't that damned old cricket drivin' you crazy?"

"Well as a matter of fact, it was you sayin', Elg you awake, Elg you awake', that I heard, not that old cricket."

"Well, sorry. Reach out and see if you can't flick eem outta there would ya?"

Elgie rolled over and stuck his hand out the window. Dead silence. Elgie rolled back over. Chirp, chirp, chirp. Elgie stuck his hand back out the window. Dead silence.

"Arliss I can't get eem! Just don't pay eem no mind and go on to sleep," Elgie said, as he rolled back over and pretended to go back to sleep.

"Say Elg, what the hell you think he's doin' anyway?"

"What I think is, why don't he quit all that cussin' and go on to sleep."

"For reals, whatcha think he's doin'?"

"Oh Arliss, you know what he's doin'. Same as he does every time he goes. He's either sittin' down there with Jack Burgess and Joe Walker and Virgil and them or he's off somewheres else. He'll be home directly."

Elgie was sitting back up now, the irritated sound in his voice gone.

"What if somebody shoots eem and kills eem and dumps eem off in a ditch somewheres?"

"Shut up that kinda talk, 'sides he ain't even workin' tonight, he's just off playin' cards or somethin'."

"You really think worms eat up Eloise?"

The thought of that had always made me scared. Used to have dreams about it right after she died.

"I don't even know what a worm eats, Arliss. She was so little though, guess it's likely," Elgie said, rolling back over towards the wall.

I'd lay there for a long time listening to that cricket and staring at the ceiling. The paint peeling an intricate pattern of lines and cracks and crevices above my head mapping out some far off planet full of drought, leaving lakes of old sunbaked clay dried hard and chipped and pried up. Moonlight stabbed through that old cypress and threw shadows all around the room. Spindly, fur-covered arms reaching in the darkness to pull you from your bed and carry you off to some real bad place. Elgie always went to sleep before me and I just had to lay there still as a corpse until I'd finally doze off.

My thoughts would drift to Daddy and where he might be and what he might be doing. I liked to imagine him off out and about doing some important lawman chores but I knew better. Not too much ever happened around here. The occasional car crash or drunk or maybe a fight but not anything too exciting. I learned much later in life that there were several forms of business that can keep men occupied until the darkest hours of the night. One and only one of which was cards. The others being of varying shapes and sizes, used in the incessant search to satisfy the needs of a man married to a woman touched and locked away in the recesses of her own mind.

"Elg, you awake? Elg?"

Chirp, chirp, chirp.

Esther sat on the front porch swinging back and forth behind a tin bucket full of apples. Long thin peelings writhed and curled around her hands like green boa constrictors trying to crush bony brown vermin as she raked the blade of the knife around the fruit exposing the greenish white meat. She held the ball in her hand and pushed the knife through its center, rotated the ball and repeated the procedure, then she scooped out the core and let it fall on to a towel by her feet before dropping the quartered sections into a small pail of water that had been cool, now tepid and full of small crescents in varying shades of brown that floated and bobbed spastically as the fresh white slices plummeted into its depths.

There was an Uncle Henry down at the hardware store that I had shown to mama one time. Now that was a knife. Just the blade was at least a good four or five inches long. The handle was bone. Hand carved bone. Yellow and black and polished smooth to where you couldn't hardly feel it in your hand. Not cheap and brittle like those butter and molasses handles on the two-bit Barlows that filled the bucket next to the cash register. The blades were shiny as mirrors and sharp as a razor and when you opened them they snapped and clicked into place. I took a piece of leather and ran the big blade down it and it sliced through just like warm butter. I didn't have to push at it at all, just the weight of the knife made a crisp clean cut. Even with all three blades open you could set it on your finger and it would just balance there, rocking gentle as a baby cradle. I had already looked at it for near five minutes when the man told me that he wanted $5.00 for it. When Elgie showed me that little Barlow that daddy got him for his birthday, it was all I could do to act like it was even a knife at all. I tried to act real excited for Elg, but I just had my mind on that knife laying in the display case.

You could have knocked me over with a feather when I looked out the window and saw Esther sitting out there. That shiny blade covered in sticky apple juice, flashing in the porch light.

"Now just where in hell might'a old nigger woman get a knife like that?"

The words fell out of my mouth and squeezed through the screen door before I could catch them and choke them back down.

"You watch who you callin' old, mister," Esther said without looking up from her work.

"Whatchu doin' up outta bed spyin' on me anyhow?"

My eyes stayed fixated on the shiny metal like a mouse staring at a loaded trap wondering how to get the bait without the slap.

"That looks like an Uncle Henry from where I'm standin', where in hell'd a old woman get somethin' like that?"

Esther stopped peeling and looked up, her head moving from side to side like a charmed snake as she snapped back, "Well if'n you'd stop callin' me old and come over here and sitcho snotty little butt down I might just let you take a look at it, might give you one or two of these apples too, uh-huh."

I stepped out on to the porch and my skin chilled and bumped up like featherless chicken skin all down my back and down my arms. I walked over and sat down next to her. The moths and aphids and flies crawled and darted at the porch lamp and I reached and slapped at a tickle on my cheek and opened my hand in the soft yellow light to reveal a little glob of guts and blood and wings that had just seconds before been a mosquito. She leaned forward and probed the blade into the bucket and pulled it back out with a apple slice stuck on its end and handed the knife to me. Even with the fruit skewered on the tip of the blade you could tell that it was very evenly balanced. I lifted the apple to my mouth and pulled it off with my teeth.

"I would say don't cut your tongue off but after the way you come out here talkin' to me, maybe I wouldn't mind so much if'n you did." Esther said. "Your daddy might not like it though if'n I let you bleed all over the front porch, so be careful with that, it's sharp." She reached up and rubbed at her eyes as she talked and in the light I could see that the nails of her hands were receded far past the tips of her fingers and her knuckles were thick and callused and strong.

"A long time ago, my daddy worked on a railroad. He was a big man so they put a hammer on him and made him a spike driver. He used to say that he could drive a spike plumb down with nothin' but two hits." She laughed and looked out across the yard. "He could tell a fib almost as big as he was too. He come home one night and he called me out on to the porch. 'Esther,' he says, 'I want you to have sumpin'.' And he reached into his pocket and pulled out this knife. I know he don't have no money to buy sumpin' like that and I ask where he to get sumpin' nice as that. He said that a train come down the track fulla railroad men all dressed in suits and ties and clean as lye soap. Said they was out there to inspect the line. Said that when that train pulled off he looked down on the ground and seen that one of them men dropped his watch outta his pocket without knowin' it and that he picked it up and ran four miles to catch that train to give that watch back. That man who dropped it was so grateful that he give my daddy that knife. To his grave he kept to that story about that knife and to this day I still don't know how him to come by it. PV been tryin' to get it offa me as long as I can remember. I done chopped off one of his fingers though when he tried to get holt of it. He don't try so hard no more."

"Bullshit," I tried to sound like I didn't much believe her but I did know for a fact that PV was missing the little finger on his left hand. I had seen the nub one time when he shook hands with daddy.

The big blade was blunt and round on the tip where it had been pulled back and forth across the whetstone and sharpened down over the years. It was really something else and before I even thought about it, I just blurted it out.

"What would you think about me maybe using this to whittle with sometime?"

"Depends on just what you plan on whittlin' with it." Esther said. "You plan on whittlin' this porch down or whittlin' on that rocker yonder then I don't think too much 'bout you usin' it at all. You plan on whittlin' down a old limb or sumpin' like that then maybe we might could work sumpin' out."

"I wouldn't whittle Mama's rocker." The thought of anybody whittling on a rocker seemed plumb stupid to me. "And, why in hell would I whittle the porch?"

"I don't know. Just seems to me, fellas your size get to whittlin' they libel to whittle anything in sight down to nothin' but a nub."

"Yeah, well, I ain't got no use for no nub anyhow." I snapped the blade back into the handle and passed it back over to her.

"PV really buy another mule to farm with?"

"Crazy old fool sure did," Esther said.

"Don't it bother you, people callin' him dumb and stuff like that?"

"Things people say don't bother me much at all. It's things people do that bother me." She clicked the blade back open and reached down and picked up another of the green apples and began to peel.

"Like what?"

I knew the things that people had done to niggras. I had heard people talk about the things that had been done to them, but I had never heard about them first hand and I thought maybe she might have a few good stories.

"Oh, things like..."

The glass shattered and crashed off the oak floor in Mama's room and rang out like a pistol shot through the window that opened to theroof just above the porch. The sounds of heartsick wailing and defiant scorn screamed out at God and the stars and heavens and everything holy.

It had been over a year since I had felt the soft tenderness of a mother's touch. The fresh white sheets soaked through with blood and sister's eyes wild and darting as she writhed and coughed and sputtered spastically, gasping for breath. Every scream vise-gripped around mama's brain like clenched hands around a wet towel wringing out the sanity like old cloudy dishwater.

I watched as they lowered her down into the hole. Her face soft and serene beneath the little glass window that would shield it from the dirt as it fell and packed in around her. The air was filled with the fragrance of flowers mixed with the scent of the fresh dug dirt piled in a mound next to the hole. Daddy just stared blank and hard at the stone. Hand cut granite carved out with nothing but a chisel and a hammer.

ELOISE ROSELLE WHITLOCK

1934 - 1936

Beloved Daughter and Sister

GO WITH GOD

I didn't think Mama was too terrible sad because she didn't cry or yell or anything that day. Matter of fact, she never made one noise at all for nearly a week. Then one night real late we were laying in the bed and she screamed the most godawful scream any of us had ever heard. Seemed like she screamed like that for a long time. She stopped screaming and took to throwing things and daddy just pulled his clothes on and left her alone. I guess it was about a week later that we noticed daddy had moved his things over to another room, the same one he slept in for years. After that Mama only screamed that kind of scream every once in a while. It'd still make you want to crawl outta your skin though.

That night on the porch we both flinched at that sound, though we had heard it before. Esther laid the knife and half peeled apple in her lap and slid her arm around my shoulder and pulled me into her side.

We sat there on the porch swing for the longest time just swaying back and forth, listening the concerto of crickets and frogs and unrepentant wrath sing out around us.

## GUPPY

**"SHOW US YOUR FINGERS GUPPY!"**

"Oh piss up a rope!" Orville yelled as he lifted the lukewarm beer off the bar and sucked at the neck. The pointy lump of gristle pumped up and down beneath the paper thin skin of his throat as he swallowed three big gulps and popped the bottle back down on to the bar.

"Come on, Gup, let's see 'em," a voice called from the back of the room.

"I said w'y don't y'all just kiss my ass! Gimme one of yer cigrets if'n you want somethin' to do," Orville stared into the mirror behind the bar and glared at the back of the room.

"Oh, here. Leave 'eem alone. He's just gonna be a ol' sourpuss is all," the man said as he walked over and handed Orville the cigarette then turned and walked back to the table from which he had come.

Orville Walters was a tortured man with webbed fingers on his right hand. Some say that he was a little off because he had lungs instead of gills and he couldn't live in the river where he belonged. Instead he had lived with his mother out in an old run-down house off a farm road in the middle of nowhere until she just up and died one day. He supposedly hated the nickname Guppy, but he answered every time somebody called him by it. He tried to join the Army one time, but he was declared a medical reject and wasn't allowed to enlist. I guess the Masons weren't as picky as the Army because they let him in. At least that's what Guppy said anyway. According to Daddy, he never went to any of the meetings and he wore a ring on a chain around his neck that had an old insignia on it. They said he had a still somewhere out in the county and that it was all that grain liquor that was rotting his brain. Nobody had ever seen his still but he had been seen in town several times buying corn, sugar, yeast and copper pipe and things like that. Maggie Wells used to say that she was his girlfriend, but he never would claim her as such. He'd tell you that she'd be anybody's girlfriend for a drink. And for two drinks she'd love you like she meant it.

Guppy sat and nursed his beer and stared a hole through himself in the mirror. He tucked the cigarette between his lips and cupped a hand around it as if to shield it from wind that wasn't blowing. He scratched a match back and forth on the bar until the friction produced flame, lit the cigarette and dropped the match on the floor and snuffed it out with the toe of his shoe.

"Y'all heard about that damned nigger sumbitch and his mules?" He was still staring into the mirror. The man behind the bar was not sure if the comment was directed at him or the men in the back of the room or if it was just meant to be thrown out there to make the world in general aware of the situation.

"Everbody's heard about it," said the man behind the bar without turning around.

"Yeah, well, maybe everybody ain't heard enough about it 'cause ain't nobody doin' a damn thing about it. Where in hell'd that wore out old black bastard get money like that anyhow? Damn." He took another drink of the beer and popped it down again on the bar.

"Aw Guppy, what in hell you talkin' about. Nobody's doin' nothin'. We're all gettin' a good laugh out of it is what we're doin'." The bartender was a short fat man with a large bald spot on the back of his head and he turned around now and looked at Guppy square in the eye as he talked.

"You know what I'm talkin' 'bout. We oughta have a meetin' and talk about teachin' some of these assholes runnin' wild around here a little respect for..." Guppy stopped in mid-sentence when he felt the hand squeeze down hard on his shoulder. He turned and saw the man that had given him the cigarette standing behind him with the two other men that had also been at the table in the back of the room.

The hand squeezed down harder into the muscle in Guppy's shoulder and he winced in the dull pain of the grip.

"Damn, Joe I's just sayin'." Once again the grip tightened and cut him off in mid-sentence.

"Ain't gonna be no meetin', Guppy," the man stared hard at Guppy.

"Awright! Awright! I's just talkin'. Let goa me!" Guppy jerked his shoulder free from the vise-like grip and rubbed at it with his hand. "Damn Joe, I's just talkin'," he said as he turned back around, shaking his head at himself in the mirror.

"Ain't nobody in here interested in what you got to say. Least not tonight anyhow. This is a bar, Guppy. It ain't no church. It's for drinkin', not preachin'," Joe winked at Guppy in the mirror and turned and made his way back to his table.

The other men turned and followed, laughing to themselves as they crossed the room. Guppy stood up from the bar and paced back and forth behind the stools.

"Aw go ahead and gimme another damned beer I guess."

He dug through his pocket and dropped some coins on to the bar and the short balding bartender popped a bottle of beer down in front of him. Within minutes Guppy Walters had made his way to the back of the room and was sitting at the table with the three men, his webbed fingers spread apart and waving about wildly in their faces.

## KLAN

HEAVY, WORN STRAPS ROLLED like black waves against a blue sky backdrop as they fell and crashed and slapped the haunches of Rosie and Jack. Rosie's hooves scratched and clawed at the hard, packed earth as the wood and metal behind her bounced off large stones and pulled back hard and resisted every inch of forward momentum. Esther watched through the window as PV inched along behind the team. She laughed at his stubbornness as he yelled and cussed his raggedy old mules. He pulled back on the reins and Jack and Rosie stopped and stomped their hooves and snorted in big gulps of thick, hot air. PV didn't know that Esther was watching him as he rubbed at the knot in his left forearm that bubbled out and crooked just below the elbow. It had been stiff and achy every morning since she had known him. He only talked about it one time when he told her about the four white boys with the black, klan blood who laid his arm out on a rock wall and held him down tight while the fifth smashed down on it with the sole of his boot, snapping it like a twig and causing it to hang limp and dangle down like a shirt sleeve with nothing in it.

It had been pretty quiet just about ever since they had moved to Texas. Her daddy had brought them here from Arkansas when she was still young. He said that he had gotten a good job, but after they moved she never did see him do much work. Just little odd jobs for white folks mainly, when he wasn't trying to be a farmer. Her mother knew the real reason they were leaving, and Esther did too when she asked her mama why they were going to Texas. She had been called a nigger so many times in her life that she couldn't remember if she had actually been called one here in Wellington. She was pretty sure that she had, but she couldn't be sure who had done the calling or how many times. That was a welcome change. People for the most part seemed decent enough here. They stayed out of her way and she stayed out of their's. PV was a strong man. He was strong enough to just walk on by. He was strong enough to swallow his own pride for the sake of his family. His babies. She loved him for that. She had often thought about the nights when her daddy would stand at the door, sometimes all night, long with that double barreled shotgun the fire light glistening off the oiled metal. The rich grain of the stock pushed tight into his armpit and his big, crooked thumb laying atop the pads of both hammers. Pacing from window to window, peeking out into the darkness. She had hidden in a shed behind shovels and rakes and sacks of feed with her mother and her brothers, and had seen through the spaces in the wooden slat walls. Her daddy standing tall on the front porch as men in white robes and hoods set fire to crosses and hung stuffed straw men with ropes from the limbs of the big oak that grew in her front yard. She had listened and watched as her own babies came home bloodied and broken, and many times she struggled to find the strength and words to encourage them to hold their heads up and trust in the Lord for protection from a mean world. Those days seemed far behind her now. Like they had all happened in another life. A life that she hovered above and looked down on and watched herself and her family stumble through.

Esther dressed in the flicker of yellow, soft and dim. The glass bulb that hung at the end of a thin string of wire coming down out of a hole in the ceiling crawled with tiny black specks, causing the light from the filament to strobe and flicker off her face. She rubbed thick salve into the scars and calluses that decorated her hands like jewelry.

Cotton. PV always said that cotton is God's way of trying to make this old rock-hard world a bit softer and a little more comfortable to live in. The last time he said that, she just said "bullshit", and he got mad and fell asleep out on the porch smoking his pipe in his rocker. She let him sit out there half the night before she went out and woke him up. Maybe he had forgotten all she knew about cotton. Planting and picking somebody else's cotton. Hands so cut up and swollen you can't hardly change your clothes without help. Wagons, sometimes ten or more, bouncing off down the road. Bales. Tons. Prices going up and up. Rich men getting more and more greedy. Busting more ground with every harvest. Mamas and Daddies picking right alongside babies. Bleeding. Bundling. Loading. Crying. Watching the wagons come back empty. Rich men smiling, pockets bulging. It had been some time since she'd picked cotton and she said she wouldn't do it ever again unless she just had to. And now there was her PV out there dragging all over. She knew before too long she would be out there crawling around again. She laughed at the thought. He always said that one day he'd get himself a piece of land and work his own cotton. Maybe even hire his own pickers.

Esther knew better than that, but she loved him too much to say so. She knew they were here. They were everywhere. They were in the banks and the feed stores.

They were in the sheriff's office. They were in the churches, even behind the pulpits. Like maggots on meat. You don't ever see them until you throw that meat in a trash can and fasten the lid down in the heat. All of a sudden there they are. Next time you look there's more than the last time. And more and more until that meat is just devoured. She knew they probably talked about him when they came out to their meetings, all white and hooded and squirmy and swarming on that old roast of hate. It never bothered him much. So far they had left him alone. PV said he could make a life around that. His dream shoved deep into his pocket as he walked among them quiet as a shadow. He knew how to fade and disappear in their presence. He was too strong to be prideful.

The front door creaked and clicked as it snapped closed. She stepped off the porch and made her way across the yard and out the opening in the fence. She looked back out across the field to see PV standing with his team pulled up tight. His left hand on his heart and his right hand waving his hat at her. She smiled and waved back as she walked up the gravel drive and disappeared in the soft darkness of morning.

"'CAUSE I NEED THE HELP, JOE. That's why. I got to have somebody around to help me with the house. I cain't cook worth a damn and I ain't gonna spend all my time doin' woman's work. Elizabeth don't look like she's ever gonna snap out of it. You got Margaret, you ain't got nothin' to worry about. 'Sides she's a good niggra, works real hard and makes about the best biscuits and gravy you ever laid teeth to," Rube said as he sipped from a little glass jelly jar.

"I guess, but what about old PV? I know you gotta have the help but you know it just looks kinda funny. Like maybe you think he's gonna make a go or somethin'. I mean, don't it bother you that everybody's talkin' about that?" Joe said, taking the jar back.

"Now how in the world would Esther workin' for me have any damn thing to do with whether or not he's gonna pull anything outta that ground of his? Esther has been around here ever since I can remember and I don't guess I give a damn what everybody's talkin' about. 'Sides she's the only one that showed any interest in the work and I got to have some help. PV's tryin' to farm that old place of her daddy's anyway and he ain't never gonna make a go of it. Never. And I don't give a frog's fat ass what everybody's talkin' about. I don't know why everybody don't just leave eem be."

"Yeah, but it just looks bad is all."

"Well, I don't guess I like it a whole lot more than you or anybody else. But there ain't a damn thing in the world I can do about it. Everybody keeps lookin' at me like there's somethin' I can do about it."

"Well you're the sheriff, they's got to be somethin' you can do."

"Like what Joe? You want me to just drive out there and start shootin'? Hell, I could shoot both his mules and him, too, for that matter. Just drive right up in the sedan and start blastin' away. Right in the middle of the daylight. That sounds like a good idea to me, don't it you Joe? Esther's the only one around here who wanted the job and I got to have the help."

"I know, I know ain't nobody bent outta shape at you. Everbody knows what shape you in. I ain't meanin' no harm to old PV I just hate to see it stirrin' everybody up is all. That's all."

"You don't think anybody 'round here would mean any harm to that old niggra, do ya? 'Cause of that damned old mule. Do ya Joe? I mean you ain't heard nobody talkin 'bout hurtin' eem have ya?"

"Well, I don't know about that. I just know it sure is stirrin' people up is all."

"Well, I guess I ain't thinkin about it near as much as everybody else."

"Well I tell you this, you might wanna start thinkin' 'bout it 'cause if he does manage to bring in some kinda decent crop you might just end up with a flash fire on your hands. I mean, sweet potatas and peanuts is one thing. Nigger cotton, well, that's a whole other story. Tell ya sumpin' else, Rube, election's just around the corner. I mean hell, you always got my vote. You know that. But some of 'em, well I just don't know. They gonna be lookin' square at you."

"Well I'll just have to piss on that bridge when I get to it."

"You gonna come out and sit in?"

"Naw, I don't think so."

"You sure? We get old Guppy lubed up enough, we all lible to make out big."

"Aw, if he's gonna be there, then hell no. I don't know how come y'all to play with him anyhow. 'Sides I ain't got any extra to be throwin' around anyway."

"Aw, Rube, he's easy pickin's. That's why. "

Joe offered Rube the jar. He took another small sip and passed it back and Joe shook his hand and turned and walked up the street.

"I'll see ya, Rube," Joe said, waving his hand back over his head as he walked away.

Rube crawled in behind the wheel of the sedan and laid his head back against the seat. The street was quiet and still. The storefronts locked and dark. He sat and listened to the buzz of Joe's truck fading in the darkness as he turned the key and the engine jumped to a smooth whine. The sedan oozed like spilled black ink through the empty street and turned and was absorbed into the blackness of the countryside.

## WHITTLE

ELGIE WAS OUT FRONT CHOPPING on an old
downed tree. He was trying to section it off so that he
could haul it away. He had been excited to get started on it
and he was still chewing on his breakfast when he ran out
the back door and went to the tool shed to get the ax. I
knew he wouldn't let me chop any, and I walked out onto
the front porch and looked out across the yard at him. He
got mad when he saw me just sitting there in the shade and
he yelled at me to do something or another but I just
waved at him, which made him even madder and caused
him to chop faster. I couldn't help but laugh at the sight of
him swinging at that stump with the little chips flying back
and bouncing off his head.

Esther was in the kitchen cleaning up the mess from breakfast when I went back inside.

"Hey Esther, whatcha doin'?"

"Now if you gonna go to all the trouble to walk in here and pull out that chair yonder and get yourself all fixed to ask me a question, then why wouldn't you take the time to come up with a better one than that? 'Hey, Esther, whatcha doin'?' I can think of a whole buncha stuff right offa the toppa my head that I'd be willin' to bet that I know and you don't," she said with a smile as she rubbed at the saucer in her hand.

"I'll tell you what," she said, "why don't you stand yourself up and walk back out that door and come back in here with a real question so's you and me can do some real talkin'. If'n we gonna talk that is." She turned and set the saucer up in the cupboard and picked another dish from the table.

I walked out on to the front porch and sat for a minute before walking back to the kitchen with my question.

"Esther, do you ever wish you was white?"

She stood without rubbing the dish and stared out at the yard and then turned and sat next to me at the table.

"Well, now, lemme see. I think that's a fair question. Pretty good one, too, 'cause I cain't remember nobody ever askin' it to me. So lemme see. Do I wish I was white. I guess I ain't really never thought too much 'bout that. But if'n I was to think about it, I'd probably have to say no."

"How come?"

"Well, I ain't too sure. Do you ever wish you was somebody else?"

"I don't guess I ever wish I was somebody else. I guess I wish a lot that I was different though."

"How you mean different?"

"Well I wish my legs wasn't funny, you know one shorter than the other and all."

"Oh I see," Esther said, looking down at my leg.

"How come it to be like that," she said.

"I don't know. It was like that when I was born. It grew but just not as fast as the other one. I was sick a lot, too, when I was real little and they said that mighta had somethin' to do with it. I don't know."

"And just what would you do if it was the same as the other one?"

"Prob'ly do a lot more runnin' and climbin' and things like that. I'd help Daddy around here a lot more, too. Help him farm, I mean. I like to help with that. He said I wasn't no count, though. Least not at farmin'. He told me to study extra hard 'cause I'd have to earn a wage with my brain some day."

"Well, do you reckon he's right?"

"Hell no. I'll do what I damn well want to when I get grown. I ain't no count. He don't know. He wouldn't know anyhow 'cause he won't let me do nothin'. 'Sides, I hate to study and read and sit around. Elgie stays on me about it too. He says, 'Arliss you wanna go around dumb as Ned in the first reader?' But I ain't dumb. I know that for a fact. Anyway, you didn't answer my question."

"Yes I did. I said no."

"Well how come? How come you don't wanna be white?"

"Oh I don't know, 'cause my mama and daddy worked too hard at bein' black I s'pose. If I was white I wouldn'tve met PV and had my kids. And just think, if I was white I never would be workin' here cookin' and cleanin' after you and you'd be the dirtiest, smelliest little scrawny thing anybody ever did see and your daddy bein' the sheriff, we cain't have that, now, can we? I mean I got to live around here too, and I don't want anybody seein' sumpin' like that, now, do I?" She laughed and swatted at me with her dishrag.

"'Sides you boys ain't half bad when you ain't runnin' and screamin' all over. I guess I'm kinda startin' to get used to ya."

"Well, I guess you ain't so bad yourself. Least you make good biscuits and gravy."

"Arliss, I tell ya, God makes things all sorts and shapes and sizes for a reason. You gonna have to be the one decides whether you just different or whether you special."

Esther smiled as she reached into her apron pocket and pulled out the knife.

"Why don't you take this on out yonder and see if you cain't find yourself sumpin' to whittle. Be careful with it now, it's sharp," she said as she handed me the knife.

"Oh I know how to handle it."

## FOOTSTEPS

THE DAYS SEEMED TO PASS TOO quickly even though I spent most of them by myself. I think I ran every square inch of that farm at least four times that summer. Every time Esther would let me borrow the knife, I'd spend more time trying to figure out a way to make her forget that she had let me borrow it than I would using it. I'd sit out there on the front porch turning it over and over in my hand, daydreaming and scheming, and never would whittle much of anything. She never did forget, though. Me and Elgie both felt the need to be by ourselves as we struggled to understand the ways of coping with loss and the separation we felt from Daddy, not to mention Mama. Elgie seemed to need that space more than I did, but I gave it to him just the same. One day I looked at him and he just looked like a grown up to me. Something in his eyes. Something serious and filled with a kind of angst that only years of living far beyond his own are supposed to bring. I had been sitting out there on the front porch when Pastor Clark from the Baptist church and three women that Daddy called Sister came up into the yard. The women were carrying covered dishes and they smiled pathetic smiles at me as the preacher asked if they could see Daddy. They went in and sat and talked about things that didn't hold my attention until they started to talk about my mama. Daddy had not talked to me and Elgie much about her, only to say that she was sick and that we should just pray for her that she would get better. Elgie wouldn't talk much about it, either, and I didn't blame him much because I knew that he really didn't know any more about what was wrong with her than I did. I guess I needed to talk about it more than they did. I heard Daddy tell the preacher that if she didn't start to show some signs of improvement that he was probably going to have to take her to a hospital and see if they could do something to help her. He said that he had done all he could do for her and she still wasn't getting any better. I thought that was a strange thing to say, seeing as how all I had seen him do for her was leave her alone. Maybe he thought that was what she needed. After that I had wanted the days to pass slower than they seemed to. I didn't want Mama to go and yet there was a part of me that felt that things would be better if she did. I tried to hide those feelings more from myself than anyone else I guess. She was my mother and I didn't want her to be sent away. Yet I didn't really want her to stay here the way she was. It felt uncomfortable. Knowing that she was always here. Locked away and doing whatever it was that she did up there. I could hear her at night sometimes, walking around when everyone was asleep. The house would be real quiet and still and I could hear footsteps in the hall and sometimes they would stop just outside of our room. I would just lay there frozen knowing that she was on the other side of the door. Not knowing what she was thinking or doing and just wishing that she would go away. She would stand out there and just cry for the longest time, and then I would hear the footsteps going back down the hall and the door to her room shut and lock behind her. I don't really remember when I stopped praying for her to get well. But I did. I stopped praying for her to get well and started praying for God to just do something with her. I prayed: "God, if you're not going to make her well, you know, make her normal again, then take her to Eloise or just take her out of here." I felt bad about that for a long time.

STUMP

SHERIFF WHITLOCK YELLED at Elgie. Made him go
get the rake and pick up ever little splinter offa the front
yard that he chopped offa that old stump. He oughtn'ta yell
at them boys like that. They good enough boys. Got half a
mind to spit in his eggs.

RABID

IT WAS UNUSUALLY COOL ON the night that Elgie ran away. Boots Conley was Daddy's deputy. He was big as a barn and round as a barrel and wore pointy, loud cowboy boots, spit- shined clear as a mirror, with his uniform. I had seen his uniform so wrinkled at times you'd have thought that he'd slept in it, but those boots were still without even a fleck of dust on them. Anybody that ever got cross with him stayed scared enough to walk clean across the street just to stay out of his way. Boots never seemed to notice though. I don't even think he knew just how big he really was, because he'd walk clean across the street just to avoid a fight. Daddy said he might be a little skittish but I knew he wasn't. He could knock a mule cold with one punch and I think he knew it too. I think that's why he steered clear of fights. Thick, white clouds bubbled in a sky crisp and blue as a sapphire and the khaki pants and shirt he wore stood out against it. I could see him next to his car that was stopped and left idling in the middle of the road. He was staring at the ground and walking back and forth in a little circle, stirring the dirt around with the toe of his boot and I crossed the yard and walked out to see what he was up to.

"Hey Boots."

"Well hey your own self, boy. Whatcha up to?" He said, still walking in the little circle.

"Come over to see what the hell you lookin' at down in the road. Saw ya from the front porch."

"I's lookin for more of that yonder," he pointed with the toe of his boot at a shiny little disc that lay half covered in the dust.

"Well I'll be, ain't that a nickel?" I bent and picked up the little disc and blew the dust off of it and rubbed it with my thumb. Boots smiled as I stuck my hand out and offered it to him.

"Stick it in yer pocket. Down in there good and deep so it don't work it's way out. Get down there and scratch around, might be there's some more," he continued to stir the dust as he talked.

"Well dadgum, yonder's some more right there."

I crawled around and picked up seventy-five cents all together and shoved it as deep as I could down into my pocket.

"You sure I can keep all this or you just tryin to set me up so you can haul me off to jail?"

"Yeah, I'd probably get promoted all the way to the top if'n I hauled you in, wouldn't I?" Boots laughed and stuck his fists up in front of him and danced around me like a boxer and tousled the top of my hair with his jabs.

"Where'd all this come from and how'd you know it'd be layin out here in front of the house."

"Your daddy got a call this mornin' and the cafe got broke into." He stopped dancing and leaned back on the car to catch his breath.

"Is that right?"

"That's right alright. They took the pinball machine right out the back door and hauled it off. I don't know how he knew but your daddy said for me to come and look out here. I found it over yonder all busted up in the ditch. I figured that they musta pushed it off the back of a truck so I was lookin' around in the road for the change. See, that's why one of these days I'm gonna give yer daddy a run for his office. On accounta I'm so damned smart," Boots winked, cocked his hat to the side and jumped off the car and danced around again, jabbing and tousling my hair.

"Got any idea who done it?" I said, as I danced back and jabbed my fists into his ribs.

"Got more than a idea," he said as he stopped dancing around and bent at the waist and put his hands on his knees and breathed heavy.

I looked past Boots and saw the busted hull of the machine laying upside down in the weeds.

"Damn. Busted it all to pieces didn't they."

"Sure did."

" Well, who done it, Boots?"

Boots looked at me and shook his head.

"Your cousin Sonny and some of that other riff raff he hangs around with."

Mama had a sister that everybody just called Sister. We even called her Aunt Sister because we didn't have any idea what her real name was. Aunt Sister had a son that we called Sonny because he wanted us to and he was a lot older than we were and most of the time when he was around we did what he said. Sonny hung the moon. That is, at least the one that followed Daddy around, anyway. Aunt Sister's husband had gone off some time ago to look for work and nobody had heard from him since. Sonny just seemed to go downhill after that. Ran all over the county at all kind of hours of the night. He played ball and Daddy said that if he kept at it it'd earn him a living one day. A lot of other people said that, too, when they saw him hit. The coach said that he would have thrown him off the team if he hadn't been so good.

My unexpected laugh took Boots by surprise and he tipped his hat back on his head and folded his arms across his chest.

"Think that's funny do ya?" he asked.

"Hell yes I do. Think it's 'bout the funniest thing I heard in a long time."

"Well just why is that?"

"'Cause now maybe Daddy'll hush about Sonny and wantin' me and Elgie to be just like him. I coulda told you a long time ago that Sonny wudn't no count. I never did wanna be anything like eem. Tell the truth I never thought much about him at all."

"Well, maybe you smart to not think too much about him 'cause if he keeps goin' like he's goin' he might just end up in more trouble than your daddy can pull him out of. By the way, your daddy said for me to tell ya'll why I's out here. He's gonna be in late tonight and asked if Esther could stay 'til he come home. Said he's got to go and do somethin' about Sonny. Anyway he said somethin' to her about it this mornin' and she said that she could, so just tell her when you see her that she does need to stay. Awright."

He danced around throwing the little jabs into my hair again before he turned and walked back to the idling car, breathing heavy beneath his shirt. I stirred around a bit more in the dirt as Boots drove off, before walking back up to the house, but I didn't find any more change.

A sink hole maybe four feet across, and bottomless as far as me and Elgie were concerned, sloshed with mud from the first hard rain of the year. I guess nobody ever noticed it forming because nobody ever said anything until a truck driving along the road fell off into it. When the driver stepped out he said he was in mud damn near up to his shoulders. I just thought he was joking until I saw it for myself. I think I could have stood on Elgie's shoulders and still been all the way under water. It was in the road near the drive of our place and I spent the rest of the afternoon dumping rock and sand and gravel and anything else that I could think of into it. As much rock as I could haul splashed down through that water and just disappeared. I wondered if it even hit the bottom, much less even started to fill it up. Without thinking about it, I had pulled off my shirt, and by the time I had gone inside my shoulders and arms and back were bright tomato-red and throbbing from the fevered sunburn. I walked to our room and fell face first into my pillow.

I woke with shivers running across my skin where the sun had scorched it. The room was still and dark.

"Hey Elg, you awake? Hey Elg, you awake? Elg?"

I stood and crossed the room to close the window and I stepped onto his bed, half to reach the window frame and half to wake him up so he could

answer a few questions that I just might have. The blankets and sheet were neatly pulled up over an old feather pillow, flat from years of his head kneading and wallering on it like a rough rolling pin working out biscuit dough. I had been sleeping so hard that I never even heard him get up.

I could hear them on the front porch as I walked down the hall. They were talking quietly and I could hear the soft slurping sounds as they sipped at the hot coffee and I could hear the chain creak as the swing swayed beneath their weight.

"Well what are you doin' up and wanderin' around?"

Esther saw me through the screen before I stepped out on to the porch.

"Come on out and sit a spell if you like. PV come to sit awhile and walk home with me when your daddy gets in. He shouldn't be too awful late. They's still some cold lemonade in the kitchen. If you want I'll get you some."

"Do you know where Elgie is?" I could feel the tears starting to well up and I didn't want to cry.

I had heard Elgie say at times under his breath that he might just run off, but I guess I never really thought he meant it. I think Daddy hurt his feelings more than he did mine. He could hurt mine, too, but I don't think as much as Elgie's. Elgie never said much about it but sometimes I could see it in his eyes. A few times when he thought I was asleep I could hear him crying. I never said anything about it though. I didn't want to embarrass him.

I think Daddy knew that one day we'd both go off from here and do things other than farming and I think that made him mad. Made him think that we thought we were better than him, like what he dreamed about giving us wasn't good enough. I think he was just scared that if he had to watch us go off and do something special and he stood by us in it, that would be kinda like admitting that there was something else other than this farm. Then he'd have to face the fact that he had spent up all his dreams on it, and all those dreams and work hadn't even amounted to enough to keep him farming. Walked off his daddy's farm and on to his own and that's as far as he ever went. Always telling people he was just being the sheriff because everybody had wanted him to be and he couldn't work the farm because of Mama. Well truth is, everybody knew he wasn't much of a farmer. And, to tell the truth, I didn't want to live the way he did. Elgie either. I guess I didn't see anything wrong in it. Most of the time I tried to do just that, to keep from hurting his feelings mainly, but also because that just seemed to be the way everybody around was. But deep down inside, I knew I wanted more for myself. Elgie too. I didn't want either one of us to end up like Daddy. Bitter and mad all the time. I wanted to do something that made me feel good and made other people feel good too. The Lord told Elgie a long time ago that if he'd just keep his eyes on him and follow the straight and narrow that he'd turn out alright. I believed that too. I didn't know if Elgie would ever end up being a preacher, I didn't know what he'd end up being but I did know he'd end up doing something important. He was special and I knew it even if he didn't.

"Whatta you mean where's Elgie? Ain't he in there sleepin?" Esther asked.

"I wouldn'ta come out here and asked if he was in there sleeping."

I didn't mean to be so smart, but it seemed to help hold in the tears.

"Well lord almighty child, where do you think he might be?"

"I think he's run off!"

"Sweet Jesus."

Esther stood from the swing and walked to the edge of the porch and stared out into the night.

"Don't get all too worked up now hun, boys got to run off and think sometimes that's all. We'll just all take a walk and see if we cain't find eem. I bet he ain't gone off too far."

PV raised his cup and took a long sip and set it on the swing next to him.

"Well, let me get my wrap, that air's got quite a chill in it tonight."

Esther stepped into the house and let the screen slam behind her. She stepped back out with her wrap around her shoulders and stepped down off the porch and turned back to see me standing on the top step.

"Well you comin' with us. I don't have no idea where that boy might be."

Esther had calmed down some as we walked along the dark road and she laughed as PV told me the story of the time he had run away after his daddy had whipped him with a razor strap for eating molasses right out of the jar with his bare hand. We all laughed when he told us how his daddy had walked in and caught him and how he had stuck his hand in his pocket and how the sticky molasses had pulled his pocket inside out when his daddy yanked at his arm. Even when he knew he had been caught, he still tried to tell his daddy that he had no idea how come molasses to be in his pockets and smeared all up around his mouth. He said his daddy whipped him more for the lying than for the molasses.

The first scream was shrill, almost feminine and canine like the yelling of a coyote. It came from beyond a cluster of trees maybe fifty yards off the road. PV stopped and listened and fumbled through the pocket on the front of Esther's apron and jolted forward into the ditch and hopped across the wire fence as the second scream was thrust out into the night. Esther turned and followed after him and I stumbled as I stepped down the slope of the ditch and fell and looked up to see her having already cleared half the distance to the trees.

Elgie was backed up against the trunk of a tall tree on the edge of the little clearing where he had been trying to camp, crying and screaming and kicking his legs at the half circle of four dogs that snarled and growled and lunged, nipping at his feet and legs. He slung about in a wild panic and the scratches on his arms and stomach revealed his attempts to climb the tree and escape the attack. Two big dogs, black and brown and short haired, barked wildly and hunched down ready to spring forward while a gray wiry haired dog with a docked tail circled from one side of the pack to the other as if standing guard. The fourth dog, a small breed with a short muzzle, yapped and ran at Elgie, snapping and darting at his legs. His pants were ripped on both legs and a steady little stream of blood trickled down beneath the torn fabric. PV, silhouetted in the moonlight, screaming and cussing and charging into the clearing. The two big black dogs backed away at the sight of the wild figure, while the third tucked his nub of a tail and vanished in the treeline. The small dog turned and yelped as PV stooped and grabbed his hind legs and in one fluid sweeping motion whisked him off the ground and bashed his head on to the rough bark of the tree trunk. A whole lot of blood and a little bit of brains came out the end of that dog's nose and he was twitching and dead before he even hit the ground. PV turned and saw the two remaining dogs beginning to inch their way back into the circle and he took two steps forward, positioning himself between them and Elgie. He dug at the handle of the knife with his thumb and he clicked the big blade open and turned it in his hand so that the blunt tip pointed toward the ground. He breathed heavy and stared calmly at the dogs. As he reached up with the back of his left hand to wipe the sweat from dripping into his eyes, the forward-most of the two dogs flinched and lunged in a flash of bright snarling fangs. PV slapped at the dog and drove the thick blade deep between the shoulders into the meat of the dog's back. The black and brown carcass slid across the dirt as it hit the ground and two more pounding thrusts of the knife were delivered to its side. He whirled around and scanned the perimeter of the little clearing and heard nothing but the deep pant of his own breathing and the sniffling and heaving of Elgie.

Esther reached down and took my hand and we walked along with PV in silence. Elgie following behind and sniffing and wiping the tears off his face and breathing quick little breaths as he limped along.

When I heard Daddy come driving in that night, I knew that he'd probably come in and give Elgie a whipping for running away like he did. I laid there for the longest time before I fell on back asleep.

Daddy never even looked in our room. Esther smiled and winked at me and Elgie at breakfast.

## GRATEFUL

I S'POSE I DIDN'T SEE NO NEED in tellin' the sheriff that the boy tried to run off. Seems to me if he got enough troubles to make him think he'd wanna run away from here, far be it for me to heap any more on eem. Tell you one thing though. I cain't remember the last time I was scared like that. Goodness gracious. When I seen them dogs out there barkin' and carryin' on, Sweet Jesus only knows. PV hadn't been there I don't know what I woulda done. Old Arliss got so white I think he was glowin' in the dark. Whitest white boy I ever seen. I don't know what I'da done if one of them boys got hurt bad or just disappeared while I was s'posed to be tendin' to 'em. They ain't no tellin' what they'd do to me. Lord Almighty. I don't know if I was more scared for that boy or me. All I know is I sure am glad PV was there, that's fo sho. I was standin' in the kitchen and sheriff Whitlock walks right up to me. "Esther," he says, "I need to have a word with you." Lord my heart jumped near right outta my mouth 'cause I'm thinkin' 'you done it now. You shoulda said sumpin. You shoulda just let that boy take his beatin and been done with it. Now look what you got into.' I walked out on to the front porch behind him standin' there shakin' while he stared out at the yard. "I want to say thank you," he says. I just keep on starin' at the floor thinkin' what in the world is he talkin 'bout. He said that Arliss had told him about what had happened with Elgie and those dogs and how me and PV went out and found him. He said that some of them dogs in that pack more'en likely rabid and that we mighta saved that youngun's life and he sure was grateful. I cain't believe he said that. I thought that was a real nice thing to say. I'm gonna have to have a talk with that Arliss too. I cain't b'lieve he went and told his daddy. I'm gon' have to remember not never to tell that child nothin' that I don't want nobody knowin'. That's fo sho. You know I guess I cain't help but feel sorry for them boys. I had all kinda things to deal with when I was a youngun but at least my mama was able to tell me she loved me ever once in a while. Daddy too. That poor woman. I cain't hold her in no judgment though. Cain't imagine losin' one of my babies. I knocked on her door the other mornin' to see if she might be needin' anything and she didn't answer so I just went on in real quiet thinkin' she might be asleep. She wudn't up in the bed and she wudn't sittin' in her chair and I got nervous for a minute. When I found her she was curled up in a ball under a blanket in the corner. I pulled that blanket back and she was sound asleep. Wet as a dishrag with sweat. I didn't know what to do with her so I just left her be. I did pull that blanket back though so she wouldn't smother herself to death. Poor thing. She sho musta loved that baby.

## FOOLS & MULES

DADDY STARTED TO GET MORE and more uncomfortable when talk shifted toward PV and Esther and the mules. It seemed to shift that way a lot, too. Seems that was all anybody could find to start off a conversation. Even the kids were talking about it. Everywhere you went, fools and mules seemed to be on everybody's tongue.

"Esther," I said, as I rounded the corner.

"Well good mornin' Arliss, whatcha know?"

"I's wonderin', you think old PV was scared of them dogs? I mean they could'a been mad is what Daddy said."

"Well now I s'pect he was plenty scared of 'em. I know I was."

"Yeah, me too. I never seen nothin' like that

though, I tell ya."

"I guess I ain't seen too much like it myself."

"Well I's wonderin', if he was so scared, how come you think he done what he did? I mean for Elgie, I mean."

"I don't guess I reckon he really thought about who he done it for. I reckon he just thought that it needed doin' is all."

"Yeah I guess so. Ya know they say that Mama's crazy as a shit-house rat," I didn't really know what else to say and that was the first thing that popped into my head.

"Well I s'pect you best watch your mouth when you talkin' 'bout your mama. 'Sides who been sayin' that?"

"Oh, just 'bout everybody that knows us, which is just about everybody I guess. They say that about PV too. Did you know they say that about PV?"

"I guess they sayin' 'bout all there is to say then ain't they?"

I followed her out the back door and across the yard to the clothesline, waiting for her to say something more about it, but she didn't.

"You think Mama's crazy?"

"Child I don't likely know. If I had to guess though, I'd say she more heartbroke than just plain ol' crazy. Wouldn't you?"

"I guess."

She pulled the pins from the fresh clothes and dropped them in her apron pocket and draped the clothes over her shoulder as she made her way down the line.

"What about PV? You think he's crazy?"

"Now old PV, he a whole other story. I might just have to agree with 'em 'bout him. Sometimes I see him out there draggin' 'round behind that team and I say the same thing, look at that old fool, he crazy as a shit-house rat."

It caught me so off guard to hear her talk like that, that I just stood there looking at her, trying to figure out if I had just heard her say what I knew I had. She stopped taking down the clothes and we both stood there and laughed until tears dripped down our chins.

"Child, let me tell you sumpin'," she said, "don't spend so mucha your time worryin' 'bout what somebody else says. Somebody told me one time they said, 'Esther, worryin' just like a old rockin' chair, it'll give you somethin to do but it won't get you nowhere at all'. Somebody told me that one time; now I'm tellin' it to you."

"Well then I don't s'pose it'd worry you too awful much to let me see that knife now would it."

She smiled and dug out the knife and handed it to me.

"Go on now and git. Lemme tend to my chores."

I spent the rest of that afternoon sitting in the shade whittling a limb about as big around as my arm down to a splinter. I had started with the grand idea of carving some nice wooden sculpture that might fill the house with some nice art, but settled on the fact that a toothpick was much more useful in this part of the country anyway.

SHACK

THEY COULD ALWAYS HEAR HIM long before they saw him. That old wagon bouncing and bucking over the hard, packed dirt full of ruts, pushed in between the weeds like snake tracks slithering through the field. It was a John Deere that he said belonged to his daddy, but it looked more like it had belonged to his great-granddaddy. People said that he had money but you wouldn't have known it to look at him. They said he had a new flatbed and a fancy Chrysler that his mother drove back and forth to town. Nobody ever saw them though. Every time Guppy showed up, he bounced across the pasture in that old beat up wagon. Came up cussing everybody for not grating a road.

He was asked one time why he didn't drive and he said that his horse always knew the way home even when he didn't.

The cabin was nothing more than an old shack, an unpainted structure about four hundred square feet, constructed from gray barn planks that sat in the middle of the pasture atop railroad-tie floor joists. It had been built by Jack's cousin Pete as a refuge from his overbearing wife. Pete had gotten himself drunker than Cooter Brown one night and had laid down on the train tracks and passed out. That train came along sometime after midnight and cut him clean in two. They found his top half in the middle of the tracks and said he looked like he was just lying there sleeping. Peaceful looking as can be and still holding on to that bottle. They found his legs in an overgrown ditch about two hundred yards down from the rest of him. Both of his shoes and socks were knocked off and nowhere to be found. His pants were shredded all apart and the buckle had been torn off his belt. Rube laughed and said that he was going to have to trade in his old watch for a new ELGIN because that gold-plated one of Pete's was still down in his pocket just ticking away. When he pulled it out it was dead on with his at four minutes past three. It hadn't even skipped a beat. They said he must have been lying right across the rail and that the wheels just sliced him clean at the waist and his belt buckle must have snagged on the train and drug his legs on up the line. The engineer must have not even seen him and he surely didn't feel the train roll over him because it was said that he didn't even slow down until he got all the way into Arkansas. Pete's wife Betty knew that Pete and Jack, Joe, Virgil and Guppy and Lord knows who else, all sat out there and drank and played cards and talked all their nonsense. She walked right up to Jack at the funeral, and gave him the old shack and told him she hoped it and him both just sat out there in that pasture and rotted away.

Jack Burgess, Joe Walker and Virgil Collins sat sipping from coffee cups that had no smoke drifting out of them as Guppy stepped from the darkness of the field up on to the crooked porch.

"What's your worry, Gup? Look like you just lost your friend and the only ones fool enough to claim ya, alla sittin' right here," Virgil said as he sipped from his cup and crossed his right leg over his left at the knee like a woman.

The fact was that when he wasn't around, none of them claimed him at all. They only let him play cards with them because everybody knew that he was a bad card player and that once he started drinking you could beat him with a whole handful of nothing. He'd get to spouting off and forget how much he had even bet and he'd just keep throwing good money after bad. Somebody would look at him just right and he'd fold every time. After he'd leave,

Jack, Joe and Virgil would all divide up his money and split it equally between them.

"Lost my whole damn town that's all," Guppy waved his arms out at the darkness in a dramatic expression of his disgust.

"Aw he musta seen PV out workin' again," Jack said as he sipped from his cup.

Virgil pulled a long, crooked cigar that looked homemade, out of his pocket. He put one end in his mouth and began to chew at it. He would continue to chew at it until he found himself nearing the end of the game and holding at least the major portion of the money that he had brought with him, at which time he would light it and blow huge clouds of smoke up at the bug covered lightbulb, disregarding the objections of the others.

"You ain't about to light that thing are ya Virg?" Joe said, leaning around to glare at Virgil.

"I just might," Virgil worked the cigar in his mouth.

"That thing looks just like a turd, smells like one too," Joe said.

"You just upset 'cause I didn't bring one for you," Virgil grinned as he chewed the mushy tip of the cigar.

"Aw hell."

"Aw leave that old fool alone, Guppy," Jack said as he sipped from his cup. "He's just a crazy old fool is all, leave eem be."

"He's makin' us all look like a buncha assholes is what he's a-doin', Jack. Everbody's talkin' 'bout it. Everybody."

"Aw hell Guppy, you don't need a old run down nigger to make you look like a asshole, you look like a asshole just fine on your own." Joe laughed as Guppy stood and glared hard at him.

Joe stopped laughing and leaned forward and glared back, "Now I don't know what's rollin 'round right now in that old twisted mind of yours, but you better change it 'cause I'll knock your damn fool head off you come at me."

Guppy's eyes darted from Jack to Virgil, who didn't say anything. Joe had never been shy about showing his dislike for him and Guppy knew that not only did he mean that he would knock his damn fool head off, but that he had often looked for opportunities to do just that.

"Aw hell Joe, y'all gimme somethin' to drink w'y don't ya. I's just talkin'."

"Aw hell give eem somethin' to drink and deal. I ain't gonna sit out here all damn night listenin' to his bullshit. Ya know, if you want somethin done about it, then do somethin' 'bout it your own damn self, and if you too chicken shit to do somethin', then for Pete's sake shut the hell up about it. None of us like it any more than you do but talkin' about it ain't doin' nothin'. Good lord," Joe said, sipping at his cup.

"I ain't no chicken shit. One of these days I might just do sumpin' 'bout it."

WATCHING

HE BENT AT THE WAIST AND knees and crept along to the edge, squatted in the high grass and leaned back, blending himself in the trees and the dense brush. Clear, oily liquid spilled out past the rim of the jar and trickled down his chin and neck. He wiped at it with the sleeve of his shirt and closed his eyes and held his head cocked to the side, stiff and still as the liquor burned its way down his throat. His body simmered uncontrollably and he lowered his head and shook it from side to side, waited and took another small sip from the jar.

The blade rattled under the wood as it bounced across the ground cutting into the sandy mixture of soil and rock and he watched the man wobble along behind, his legs flailing beneath him like a marionette. He squinted his eyes at the figure that moved along blurry in the bright sunlight in front of him and sat still as the clatter of the reins and bridles and the calling out of PV grew louder and louder, nearing the edge of the field before turning back and softening again.

"C'mon now nice and slow. Cut that ground so the cotton grow. Make a man old for he get rich, least he be a free poor ol' sumbitch. I say hey now. Say C'mon now."

He talked to himself and shifted in the brush and sipped continuously from the jar, shuddering and shaking his head as he watched the man and the team distort in the vaporous heat and absorb into the landscape only to emerge again, growing clearer and louder and louder before turning back to the field leaving thin wakes of deep rich scars in the earth. He breathed, slow and deliberate, as he stared out from the trees. A thick vein slithered under the skin at his temple and throbbed and pulsed and writhed like a gorged worm when he bore down on his back teeth and grinded them together. Blood rushed hot and fast into his brain and he cussed the man as he stood to his feet and swayed in the dizziness and batted his eyes at the bright flashing spots that danced in them. He staggered along as he made his way back into the thicket from which he had come, stopping now and then to lean against a tree and catch his breath and sip again from the jar.

## LUTIE

DADDY SAID THEY BEAT UP a niggra boy over at
Lutie one night. Said whoever done it kicked that boy in
the balls until they almost swelled up and burst. The boy
told the sheriff over there that he had been trying to walk
across a creek on a downed tree and he slipped and busted
his own balls. I guess they believed him because they didn't
ever do anything about it. Esther didn't think anybody was
looking at her when she closed her eyes and mouthed out
the words 'sweet Jesus', but I was. The first person that
came to my mind was Sonny. I had heard him cuss negroes
before, even threaten them a time or two, and it made me
feel a bit queasy to think that somewhere out there, blood
that had once mingled with my own had soured and spoiled

to the point of such hatefulness. I watched Daddy sip his coffee and rattle the pages of the newspaper. I didn't know why he'd just come out and say something like that right in front of Esther. It almost seemed like he just wanted her to know. Wanted her to know that somewhere out there folks were still beating up niggras every once in a while and just because we were polite to be around, didn't mean that they weren't. Esther looked almost shocked when I asked Daddy why. Asked him what that boy had done to them to get beat up so bad. He just shrugged his shoulders and said, "Hell I don't know." He didn't even look at me when I asked why then did they beat him like they did. He just kinda shook his head the way he did when he heard something that he considered to be stupid enough not to deserve any kind of reply. Elgie just looked at me like I was touched. Esther just kept on doing what she was doing like she hadn't been listening. I guess that's what she was supposed to do. I wondered if Daddy had ever beat up a niggra and not known why he'd done it. I thought that he more than likely had, and I wanted to say how silly that sounded to me, to just whip somebody for no reason, but I never did. I just sat there. I felt bad for not saying anything. I wanted Esther to know that I thought that was silly but I never did say so.

## POISON

A TINY LITTLE ORANGE SPECK glowed bright and faded in the blackness that separated the trees just beyond the fenceline. A few seconds later it glowed and faded again and continued to do so in an almost rhythmic cadence for about five minutes then abruptly stopped. A flash of yellow danced behind the faint outline of two cupped hands, jumped at the darkness and disappeared leaving behind the little orange speck to once again resume its cadence.

The moon high, faint and thin like a giant thumbnail floating in a drum of old motor oil, yielded little, if any, light at all. A tall silhouette high-stepped cranelike from the treeline, stopped and looked around then continued on down the edge of the field stepping over bed after bed until it had aligned itself with the row that offered the straightest path to a pen, hidden from the house by what PV called his barn. Four strands of wire prickled with barbs, stretched taut between posts of once promising young trees cut to sections and now serving as amputeed sentries speckled with round scars.

The scent of the man wafted out on the air ahead of him and drifted into the nostrils of Rosie as she stood in the back corner of the lean-to. Heavy-eyed and sore from ten long hours of pulling the rickety one-row planter with the dull blade as it scraped and pried the dirt and bubbled up the ground behind her. There was a scent, an odor of fear that she had smelled many times on men as they approached animals and it was so faint this time that its presence did not alarm her and she continued to give in to the heavy eyelids as they slammed shut, each time pausing just a little longer before prying them back open.

"Ho mules," the man whispered as he approached.

Rosie stomped her hind right foot at a fly causing the man to flinch and he whispered at her again.

"I said ho mule, you keep 'er quiet now, hear me."

The short bay gelding mule named Jack that always lagged half a step behind, causing Rosie to bear most of the strain of the yoke, stepped from the side of the lean-to, dropped his ears back on his neck and peered cautiously at the figure. The smell of nervousness was also not uncommon to him, but the thought of pulling at this hour seemed a bit much to ask and he stomped his front hoof and snorted a warning of revolt.

The man pulled a worn pair of leather gloves from his front pocket and worked his hands deep inside them, opening and closing his fists to insure that his fingers had filled every last bit of their staggered pouches. He then took his right foot and stepped on the second wire, grabbed the remaining top two wires in his right hand and pulled them apart to create an opening. He bent down and stuck his left leg through the hole. Then his head. As he pushed his way through the opening and tried to step into the pen, one of the barbs caught his shirt and tore it from the collar all the way down to the waist.

"Well son of a bitch," the man said, twisting and contorting his body in an attempt to examine the damage.

"This was a damn good shirt too, you stupid ass."

In his swearing at Rosie he realized that his voice had gone from a gentle whisper to a tone that might just carry in the night breeze.

"Ho now mules," he whispered again, fearful that his tone might spook Jack.

As he crawled on through the wire fence and stood to his feet, Rosie caught a flash of silver out of her half closed eye and turned to see the man holding a small tin can. The can was covered with a piece of burlap bound tight around by twine. She had seen PV carry similar cans that he had filled with honey or molasses to pour on their feed. It made the corn and oats taste sweet, and she perked her ears and turned, now fully alert to face the stranger.

A large drum that had been cut in half and attached to eight three-foot two-by-fours stood on the back wall serving as a feed trough for the mules. As he approached the stall, the dark figure pulled at the twine, letting it fall to the ground. He then crumpled the burlap in his hand and poked at his back pocket until he was convinced that the rough, wadded fabric was secured. He paused for a moment, looked at Rosie and patted her on the forehead between her eyes as he made his way to the trough.

The man then turned the can upside down and a grayish white powder floated down and sprinkled over the grain that leveled the curve in the bottom of the drum-half. He tucked the can in his left armpit and pulled a flat, flask-like glass bottle from the bib of his overalls. Rosie walked up behind him and nudged at his back as the rich, brown liquid oozed from the bottle and dripped down into the trough. The sweet, unmistakable smell of molasses overpowered the strange scent of the powder and she was now convinced that this dark, nervous intruder was more friend than foe. She nodded her head up and down as he ran his gloved hands under the feed, coating it with the sticky mixture.

Once the procedure was done, the man rolled the gloves from his hands, and stuffed them into the can. He walked to the corner of the stall, peered around at the house, then darted back to the barbed wire fence. He tossed the can over and again stepped and pulled on the wire. As he stuck his head and shoulders through, he arched his back in a dramatic bend in an attempt to keep the barbs from further damaging his already ruined shirt. He managed to escape unsnagged and ran in a full sprint out across the middle of the field and disappeared in a fluid shadow sucked up by the blackness of the waiting treeline.

Rosie laid her ears back and snorted and kicked at Jack as he rounded the corner and attempted to approach the trough. She had decided that after another day of his laziness, she was the one who deserved this unexpected treat and tonight she was determined to make that clear. Jack nipped at her haunches as she stood and chewed at the feed and with her hind leg she delivered a kick that caught him dead center in the breast and he bellowed and neighed and jumped whimpering back around the corner.

One single ray of sunlight shot through a knot hole in the top of the stall and pierced her eye like a white hot needle. Sometime before morning she had felt the uncontrollable buckling of her front knees, her head begin to spin and her face bounce hard off the side of the trough before it slammed into the hard packed earth. Instinct pulled her back up only to let her fall a second and third and fourth time. She lay in the cool dirt on her side. Still. Glazed over. Her tail lay motionless on the ground as flies buzzed and bit and pestered at her. A large puddle of urine foamed and soaked into the ground under her hind legs and the lower half of her abdomen. Her breath was slow and deliberate and the swelling from the burning gases that ate away at her insides had already begun to give her once lean girth a tight, grotesque shape. Jack walked from the far edge of the pen and stepped into the lean-to. His nostrils flared at the scent of death that lingered and his hooves scratched and clawed at the ground as he violently backed out of the stall and pranced in a fit around the small pen, whining and snorting a plea for help at the air and clouds and trees and anything else that lay within his sight.

# OTIS USSERY

PV SAT ON THE EDGE OF THE bed and yawned and rubbed warmth into his crooked arm. His back was stiff and achy and he pushed his stomach out towards the wall and his chin up towards the ceiling, arching and twisting and limbering himself. Esther lay on the bed on her side facing away from him. The quilt pulled up tight under her chin. She stirred as PV stood up and threw his half of the blanket up over his pillow.

"You want coffee, hun?" he said, without looking at Esther.

PV laughed at the low growl that drifted from beneath the quilt and resonated in the room. His overalls lay in a crumpled pile at his feet and he stepped into them and pulled the soft denim up his torso, threw the straps over his shoulders and buckled them to the bib and walked off through the darkness. Esther could hear him clanking around in the pots and pans and the aroma of coffee drifted down the hallway and flooded her room and seeped into her lungs, bittersweet like gasoline pumping through the lines of a small block engine, stirring and warming it into motion. Five heavy steps dragged across the floor and the door popped twice off the frame as he stepped outside and let it slam behind him. Esther stirred beneath the quilt as she made a half-hearted attempt to pry herself from the grip of the fresh sheets. It was still early and she knew that she could make the walk to the Whitlock house in just over an hour. Sheriff Whitlock wouldn't be leaving for at least another three hours and those boys wouldn't be grumblin' around 'til God knows when. If she walked fast, she could still get a bit more sleep and still make it in time to fix some kind of breakfast. She rolled back over and kneaded her head into the pillow. Esther blinked and then blinked again to notice that forty minutes had passed and she jumped from the bed in a panic and began yanking at her hair and clothes. She cussed herself under her breath for not getting up and having coffee with PV. Now she wouldn't have time to have any at all and that did not set well with her. Coffee was something that she seemed to need more and more as time went by, and on the mornings that she did not have it the miles between her house and the Whitlock house seemed to stretch beneath her feet. She was dressed and out the door within ten minutes. She looked around but saw no sign of PV near the yard or out in the field.

"I'll just let the wind carry you one this mornin'," she kissed her right hand and slung it up over her head in a sporadic circle and shuffled out of the yard and down the road.

She was half skipping and half walking as she made her way up the yard and she was panting and primping as she slung the screen back and darted into the kitchen. Cool water pooled around her lip and dribbled past the rim and ran down her chin and neck and diluted the sweat that beaded on her chest as she gulped from the glass. Within minutes the sounds of the metal fork tinkling in the bowl whisking and fluffing the eggs and the smell of sausage crackled through the kitchen. She had been in such a hurry when she came up that she hadn't noticed Elgie sitting on the front porch. She could hear Sheriff Whitlock mumbling under his breath as he made his way up the hall pulling the holster tight around his waist and pushing the pin of the buckle through the fourth hole in the belt. He breathed deep and held it before letting the breath expel outward causing his stomach to bulge just over the top of the buckle. Twisting his back, he bent at the waist and pulled the belt again, releasing the pin and slacking the cinched leather. He looked down and mouthed one, two, three as he counted the holes. The pin wedged into the second hole on the belt as he shook his head and took another deep breath.

"Good mornin', Esther," he said as he stepped into the kitchen.

"Mornin'," she said, smiling and trying not to look flustered.

Somedays it seemed like just as fast as she had said good morning she was saying goodnight and walking back off towards her home. That day got away before I could even do any whittling. I had almost gotten to where I hated to see her go. Elgie too. She smiled a lot and that was nice to see around here.

The lightning bugs blinked neon green around her face. The evening air was cool and damp, and it burned in her lungs as she breathed in deeper and deeper with every step. A narrow trench stretched out alongside the road and the grass swayed as the crickets and bullfrogs croaked and chirped back and forth shielded in the growth. It was a clear night and the stars punched tiny bright pinholes in the black canvas that covered everything as far as she could see. She walked past pastures lush and green and speckled with cows and calves that stooped and pulled at the ground, ripping out the tender grass and pulping it in their jaws.

Fluffy, white balls of cotton glowed in the fields beneath the moon and she laughed at the thought of crawling around picking it next year.

The house was open and dark and still as she stepped through the front door and hollered.

"Hun, you here!"

"Hun, I'm home!" she yelled again.

She stood in the silence for a moment before stepping back out on to the porch.

"Now I just cain't believe that you'd just go off and leave everything just standin'. This just like you, Otis Ussery. Just like you."

She talked to herself as she moved to the edge of the porch and looked out towards the back.

"PV!" she called again and stood still in the silence.

She walked back inside and set her things down and stood again in the stillness. She walked from room to room and turned on the lights and pulled the curtains and called for him. She looked for him like a mother looks for a small child. She even knelt and looked under their bed. PV was a grown man but he had been known to tease her like a schoolboy. She walked into the kitchen and took down a glass and drank it twice filled with water before setting it down on the counter.

Jack rounded the pen and saw the lights on in the house and whinnied out. Esther heard his neighing but ignored him. He continued his nagging until she could stand no more and she stepped back out on to the porch and yelled into the darkness in the direction of the pen.

"Shut your stupid ass, you stupid ass!" she giggled at herself and sat down in the rocker.

She enjoyed sitting out at night and she half expected to see PV come shuffling up the road holding some dead, dripping varmint by the tail. It had been a long day and she drifted off in the comfort of the rocker. She had slept almost two full hours when Jack peered back around and spotted her and starting the nagging again. She grumbled as she stepped off the edge of the porch.

"I cain't believe that old fool'd go off a-huntin' or wherever he is and leave me to feed you old ignorant stinky beasts. I tell you, Jack, I wouldn't wanna be in his shoes when he come walkin up on me tonight. And if'n he think he gonna try the sweet talk on me askin' me 'honey cain'tcha just whip me up somethin' quick, I's starvin over here and ain't no cookin like yo cookin',' uh-uh, not tonight 'cause I am too, too tired for that," she giggled again as she made her way across the yard to the pen where Jack pranced and watched her.

She pulled the wire apart and crawled through into the pen. Jack nudged her with his nose and she pushed him back with a slap just below his eye. She walked to the trough and saw that it was plenty full of fresh water and she turned and moved toward the stall. She saw the outline of Rosie lying in the blackness and a lump stretched across her girth that looked like a draped and wadded tarp. Her heart pounded as she stepped into the lean-to and saw the soles of his boots protruding from the darkness. She cocked her head and stared at the pile. Frozen.

"PV? Hun?" she laughed nervously at the realization before her as she stepped towards him.

"PV?"

"You crazy old fool what in the world you doin out here sleepin with this old mule."

She knelt down beside him and rolled him over on his back and pulled him up into her lap and pressed his face to her breast.

"I done told ya now. Wake yourself up, hear? Wake yourself up!" She pressed her cheek to his face and screamed as the tears streamed from her eyes.

"Oh sweet Jesus! Oh my lord, sweet Jesus, don't take eem please don't take eem from me! Wake yourself up right this minute! You wake yourself up Otis Ussery! Oh sweet Jesus!"

She screamed and cried until she could no longer and she laid back against the swollen stomach of Rosie and held his body to her and stroked and kissed his face while Jack brayed and pranced around the stall.

## JUST DRIZZLING

"WHY IN HELL ARE THESE EGGS crunchy?"

"Shut up and just eat your breakfast Arliss," Elgie said without looking up.

"Scrambled eggs ain't s'posed to be crunchy Elgie. I know that to be a fact and these scrambled eggs are crunchy. Esther!"

"She ain't here Arliss. Now hush and just eat your breakfast, or go on."

Elgie pounded his fist on the table and glared.

"Whatta ya mean she ain't here. Esther?"

"I'm tellin' you she ain't here. Daddy made breakfast 'fore he left this mornin'. Esther won't be back for a while."

"How come she ain't here? Whatta ya mean she won't be back for a while? She ain't quit has she?"

"Naw. Daddy just let her stay home a while."

"How come?"

"Well you was already asleep, but Daddy told me that PV died."

"Died? You mean he's dead, dead?"

"Yeah, he died. Daddy said he had a heart attack or somethin'. Anyways he's dead and Daddy told me that he was gonna let Esther stay home for a while, 'til he gets buried and everything."

"Are you shittin' me Elgie? Is PV really dead or you just shittin' me?"

"No Arliss, he's really dead. Daddy told me."

"What'd he die from?"

"Daddy said that he mighta had a heart attack or somethin'. Now stop askin' me 'cause that's all I know about it."

"Damn. I cain't believe he's really dead. Damn. Elg, how come him to have a heart attack?"

"Damnit Arliss, hush and leave me alone! I said that's all I know about it. Now eat your breakfast or go on!"

"Gees Elg, you ain't gotta be such a shitass about it. I's just wonderin', that's all."

Elgie slung back his chair and the screen door slapped with a crack behind him as he went outside.

I sat there in the jarring quiet and ate those eggs, crunchiness and all. Everything seemed so quiet. I heard birds chirping and dogs barking and leaves rustling in the trees but it still just seemed so quiet. I felt the butterflies fluttering in the pit of my stomach and a sadness fell on me cold and damp as a drizzling rain. Just drizzling. Not hard enough to do any good. Just gray and sticky enough to make you wanna stay inside. I didn't know how long she would stay gone. What I did know was that Daddy treated death and its effects on the living with a reverence with which he treated very few other things and she would more than likely stay gone a while.

## CRAZY OLD FOOL

I REMEMBER THE FIRST TIME I EVER saw him. Wudn't big as nothin'. Skinny as a string. Looked like a little burnt twig draggin' along behind that old cult'vator cussin' old widow Bertram's half dead mule. I laughed 'til my sides was hurtin', tears runnin' down my face. He looked over and saw me watchin' and he took off his hat and tipped it. I thought to myself, 'look at that fool tippin' his hat at me. Like he was somethin' special. Like I was just s'pose to stand there and swoon over him in that hot sun. Next thing I know he's standin' out in the yard talkin' to Daddy in a clean white shirt and smellin' like lavender soap and I'm a-goin' off with eem. First time he tried to get on me I slapped the tar outta him. Slapped eem so hard his teeth rattled. He looked like he was gonna cry. I figured it out though. Figured out that's where babies come from too. Figured that out the hard way when Oran come out feet first. Big feet too like his daddy's. Figured out it's all parta lovin' somebody. Ain't too hard to love a good man. Easy to love a real good one. Drug myself all the way back to where I started from just for him. I thought that when Daddy died that would be the last of this old place. Never thought he'd wanna take it and try so hard to do what Daddy never could. I sulked around for days when we moved back in here. All them memories still hangin' in the air. You could still see the spots on the wall where Mama had her pictures hung. I hung mine in the same places on the very same nails. Didn't change the memories. Just the faces in the frames. After three or four days PV come in and said that Mama would be ashamed to see me actin' like I was actin' and I knew he was right, and I swept off the floors good and hung some things around tryin' to brighten it up and slowly but surely we started pushin' those old memories right out the back door. Guess I cain't blame the boys for not comin' home. They daddy knew that they loved eem and they knew that he loved them too, Lord knows he wudn't afraid to tell 'em and they knew that he wouldn't want them to come all the way back out here just to see eem put down in a hole. He raised them up not to give too much thought to death. Just move on through it like mud.

Everybody gonna live and everybody gonna die. Just let the ones you love keep knowin' you love 'em and everything'll be alright. When we all get to heaven, what a day of rejoicing that will be. I hope he knows I loved him. He's prob'ly sittin' up there lookin' down on me and laughin' right now for me thinkin' about all that. Crazy fool laughed all the time. I remember one time when his mama's sister's boy got killed. He's maybe twenty at the time and ridin' on a horse and a snake spooked it and it run eem up under a tree and broke his neck on a low limb. Craziest thing anybody ever heard of. PV said if that ain't Jesus callin' you home then I don't know what is. We went around to the house and they had eem in the back room propped up in the bed on some pillas sittin' up. PV and some of his cousins got to drinkin' and messin' around and they sneaked back to where he was. They laid out some sweet patatas 'cross that boy's lap and pulled the bed out and squatted on down behind it. Pulled his other arm back by his head and laid a sweet patata right up in his hand. One of 'em come around and told me to go on back there and make sure it wudn't gettin' too hot in that room. Said they didn't want eem to go to stinkin' 'fore they could let everybody see eem. Made sense to me, so I just walked on back there. When I opened that door PV knocked that boy's arm down and that sweet patata come flyin outta his hand and plopped down on to the floor right in fronta me and I looked and saw them other sweet patatas layin 'cross that boy's lap and I screamed bloody murder and run down that hall and shot out across that yard and I never did stop or even look back 'til I was home. I was just sure as I could be that that boy had come back alive. PV come walkin' up still laughin' his damn fool head off. I laughed too, but not for a few days and not 'til after I slapped a good knot on toppa his head. He was even laughin' when the knot come up. That's just the way he was I guess. He was prob'bly laughin' layin' out there by that old dead mule too. Laughin' 'bout sumpin' he found funny 'bout droppin' dead. That's the way his mind seemed to work. Thinkin' back, I cain't remember one time I ever saw him get mad. Laughin' all the time.

Crazy old fool.

## LAID IN STATE

**HE'D ALREADY LAID IN STATE** for a whole day when we got there. Her brother Everett had started on the box, but he was a poor carpenter, and a three-sided structure with corners that fell somewhere between forty-five and ninety degrees lay undisturbed in the front yard amidst a pile of soft curls, creamy and golden, like fresh-cut little pats of butter where they had been peeled from the planks and fallen and piled up on the ground around the coffin. Everett walked around the side of the house and yelled at three other men who were standing in a half circle passing a jar full of clear liquid back and forth.

"I sure could use a hand with that box yonder. I cain't hold on to it 'nough to git it squared up where the top'll lay flush."

The drapes were pulled together, overlapping to keep the house dark and cool and still. We could see his feet from just inside the front door. They were long and thin and bony and they stuck up under the sheet, stiff with rigormortis, like two tent poles holding up the printed fabric. Esther sat sleeping in an armchair, red-eyed and tear-stained. Daddy walked soft towards the kitchen careful not to wake her. He found a large, warm pie sitting on the counter and with a knife that looked big enough to field dress a deer he cut two small slices and laid them on a cloth napkin. He cut a third piece as big across as his fist and poured coffee from the stove into a cup, stained a dull beige in its well and chipped just around its rim.

"S'pose ya'll wanna walk back there and look at eem. Best to do it now while ain't nobody here. Go on if ya want to then take this pie on outside. I'm gonna visit with Everett some." Daddy handed me the napkin and took his coffee and pie out to the front porch.

"Hey Elg, I don't reckon I care much about seein' him do you?"

"Aw come on Arliss, I'll go back there with ya. I wanna see what a dead guy looks like. Cain't be that bad. They probably just look asleep is all, come on I'll go with ya."

He was laying there still as could be. He looked like he was just sleeping but he was sitting up pretty straight, the sheet pulled around his waist. The hair from his stomach poked through the gaps in the nightshirt where the buttonholes stretched to meet the buttons like weeds growing up through railroad ties. His hands folded on his lap, nails long and yellow with thin black lines caked under them. His lips had fallen apart, giving him the appearance that he had been frozen in mid-sentence. Eyes closed as if concentrating, finding just the right words to get across the point that he was trying to make.

"Well I think I've about damn near seen enough. I'm goin' outside. How in hell am I s'pose to eat pie after seein that mess." The little bumps on my arms and up my back still crawled over my skin and I could feel my Adam's apple jumping in my throat as I choked back the tears that had begun to well up in my eyes.

I took the napkin and walked outside and sat down on the back of our truck. Elgie came runnin' out right behind me.

"Wait up Arliss, you got more pie than me."

"Ya know everybody dies, Arliss," Elgie said, chewing at his the pie.

"I ain't dumb Elgie, I know everybody dies. Don't mean everybody wants to come along and see it is all."

"Just think though, now you seen it. Once you seen one dead guy you pretty much seen 'em all I guess." Elgie wiped his mouth on his shirt sleeve as he chewed.

"Didn't you think he was just gonna sit up and say somethin'?"

I looked at Elgie hoping he might open his mouth and drop out something that might make me feel a bit better about death, but he just stared off across the yard.

"Yeah, looked like he might just sit up and yell GIT THE HELL OUTTA MY ROOM!" Elgie grabbed my arm as he yelled and I jumped and dropped the last bite of my pie.

"You butthole, you done made me drop my pie!" I tried to sound mad but I couldn't help laughing.

Elgie handed me what was left of his slice of pie.

"Here, eat the rest of mine if you want it,"

"W'y hell, that ain't nothin but crust, eat it your own damn self."

The sun had begun to sink and the sky burned pink and tinted everything in and beneath it. The clouds dense and scattered, fluffy, giant clumps of cotton candy floating just out of reach. We sat and watched neighbors and far off distant kin trickle into the house in a steady procession of black, only to emerge removing their masks of somber expressions to reveal socialite smiles. Men stood in the front yard and smoked and talked about baseball and money and farming and never said anything about dying or the dead. Women shuffled in and out of the house and sipped lemonade and coffee from the front porch. Everett and the other men pried and hammered at the pine until it started to take on the shape of a primitive rectangle. PV had told Esther, some time ago, that if he should ever get killed to bury him in a coffin hand-hewn from soft ponderosa pine and not to lay him in some box that would put her in debt. He said all he needed was to carry the blame of leaving her destitute into the afterlife. "I'm gonna have a helluva nuf trouble talkin' my way up through those pearly gates as it is and besides that, I'm sure that once I get up there I'm gonna need a little cheerin' up. And I know I'd get a good laugh outta watchin' your lazy ass brothers tryin' to build me a box fit to lay in," he'd say. That was always one thing that she seemed to agree with him on. Why spend all that money on some fancy casket. The dead ain't gonna care and you can't admire it under six feet of packed down dirt. She loved him, but as far as she was concerned you could wrap him in an old sheet and drop him in a hole. That old, worn out body in there wasn't him anyway. He was gone. His soul was gone and at peace resting in the hand of Jesus.

## FRIEND

I BARELY KNEW HIM, BUT AFTER we got home that night and everybody was asleep, I went out on to the front porch and sat down on the swing and cried. I don't really even know why but I did. I cried like I did after Eloise died. I cried for Esther. It's hard to see a friend hurting. I think that's when I realized that she was my friend. Maybe I just missed Mama too. Missed the way things had been. The way things were supposed to be when you're just a kid. Daddy didn't seem to be very upset about it at all, and I couldn't help but think that maybe he was glad PV was dead. Just one less nigger for him to worry about.

## RUBAL

THE SWEAT BEADS GLISTENED on his face like a thousand tiny diamonds scattered in the loose folds of a black, velvet feather pillow, orange and yellow and jumping where the fire light danced among them. The stiff, prickly grass hairs dug into his neck just below the jawbone. The furthermost tip of the big toe on his right foot pushed hard against the earth, his left leg bent at the knee kicking and fanning the air and stretching and arching his back, his chin jutted up at the night air in a futile attempt to slack the rough, braided grass that draped over the bare limb and wrapped around the trunk of the lifeless Cottonwood. His tongue swelled with the tightening of the rope and he gagged on the purple lump of flesh as it thickened in his mouth and forced its way out to dangle toward his chin. Tears burned in his eyes and he could feel the bulging behind his eyelids as he clamped them shut. Sticky warmth ran down his wrists and through his fingers like thick molasses dripping down from where the barbs cut into his flesh and rubbed against the bone. The laughter of two figures silhouetted in the firelight, flowing ghostlike in their robes and the white pointed hoods jutting up toward the heavens, pounded in his ears as the stench of his own excretions soured in his nostrils. The makeshift pulley slacked as the two figures stood, releasing the rope from the tension of their body weight.

A sharp sting slapped across the base of the boy's neck just below his skull and he looked up to see his father standing above him. A huge shadow towering and ranting and raving, hot steam floating on the whiskey in his breath and billowing out into the darkness, a dragon awakened from a deep sleep, disoriented and coughing kerosene and brimstone. His hands laced together at the fingers and squeezed the smooth bone grips of the gun. He raised it until the bead at the end of the barrel was once again trained on the middle of the thickest part of the heaving mass that stood with both feet now flat on the ground some five yards beyond his sights. He felt the rumble in his stomach as the negro in front of him looked square into his eyes and smiled and he felt the tears well and run down his cheeks as he lowered the pistol and looked away.

"Shoot that lumpashit, Rubal! Shoot eem this goddamn minute!" The man bent and screaming into the boy's face.

The boy wiped at his eyes with the back of his hand. His father slung his arms in the air as he walked away toward the others.

The two flowing figures sat back down on the slack that was tied to the base of the tree and the rope once again pulled tight across the limb easing the man up to the height where the furthermost tip of his toe stabbed and probed at the ground just inches out of reach. He could feel the joints in his neck and down his back begin to separate and pop as muscle and nerve and cartilage stretched against the pull of gravity. The heavy grass braids burned as they tore the skin around his neck. A guttural grunt pushed through the constricted airways sounding like the snort of a small pig. He could hear the laughter ring out behind him once more and he closed his eyes and made another futile stab at the hard packed earth. He thought of all the miles he had walked in his lifetime. He thought of the times when he was just a boy, walking. How he wished time after time that he could just sit and ride and hang his feet just inches above the ground and watch it roll by beneath him. His body made another instinctive stab at the ground and he felt the sharp pain shoot down the back of his skull and the ache wash over him, hot like fresh bacon grease frying and sizzling the muscle before seeping out and scalding his skin. He could no longer feel his body, though he knew that it jumped and lunged and amused until his legs jerked and twitched and then became still, swaying back and forth like a giant plumbline.

The fist, hard and heavy as a twenty pound sledge on a hickory handle, crashed down on the middle of the boy's back and the revolver slung to the ground and embedded itself in the loose dirt and dry, yellow grass that rustled just below his knees. The tears etched little white lines down his dirty cheeks as the stings of the open palm crashed against them. His father's yelling and cursing inaudible beneath the pounding blows and loud, hollow ringing that followed.

One of the flowing figures walked toward them and spoke, waving his arms above his head. The ringing began to subside, but the boy still could not make out what the man had said to his father.

"Shut the hell up, Seth! If he cain't shoot one goddamn nigger then what the hell count is he! I'll be damned if'n I'm gonna raise no little nigger lovers!"

The slap slammed into his brain again and rang out louder than before. His eyes stung as the salty tears flushed them. A fine crimson mist sprayed off his lips as the warm blood flowed in a steady stream from both of his nostrils.

The opening at the end of the barrel wedged into his ear and forced him down, pinning his head to the ground. His father stood possessed above him and twisted the revolver until the sight on the end of the barrel cut and tore and cut a trench into his ear canal. The hammer clicked three times and slammed down on the empty chamber and his body shuddered as the hammer clicked again, rotated the cylinder and slammed again on to another hollow chamber. The man pulled the hammer back and clicked it one last time into the boy's ear and then stood and threw the pistol down hard against his temple.

"Damn thing wasn't even loaded you little sissy."

The dull thud of the metal shot through his skull and numbness ran down into his arms and hands. He had felt the same pain before when the man had slammed the thick arthritic knuckles into the soft tip of his nose. Coarse leather covered the worn toes of the man's boots and like rough sand paper on soft green pine, they scratched and gouged as they punched the tender flesh of the boy's belly where his shirt had hiked up exposing his torso. Through the aching and ringing and pounding he heard the sound of the hinge squeak, the truck cough and sputter, and the slow idle grow to a tormented whine that moaned as it faded into the darkness of the pasture. He pulled his knees up to his chest and hugged them and rolled over on to his side to face the pendulum that hung beneath the limb. His head jerked against his knees as he buried his face in the worn fabric of his pants and sobbed and heaved with the moans and howling of deep longing.

## LONELY THING TO DO

HE SAT AND FINGERED A SMALL silver locket, plain in its design and worn smooth from years of the thick calluses of a laborer's thumb and palm and fingers rubbing back and forth across its top. With his thumb Rube pushed the stem protruding from its side. The top sprung open and popped into place erect behind a shield of crystal, which bubbled above the crisp black numbers and needle sharp hands that ticked around the surface. He rolled the serrated edge of the stem between his thumb and index finger and snapped the lid closed. He stopped himself just before pushing it back into his pocket and he paused and rolled it over in the palm of his hand.

ALL MY LOVE, LIZZIE etched the back surface of the watch and he stroked it before wedging it back into the pocket of his pants.

He closed his eyes and laid his head back and thought about her, remembering the way she was when they were young. He didn't like to, but sometimes he just couldn't help it. There was a time when just being in her presence could make him feel drunk. Dizzy and light headed and faint from her touch. He wondered what she could possibly be doing up there. What was she thinking? Or was she even thinking at all? He used to yell at her, loud and cruel, that the baby was gone but he and the boys weren't and that they had needs. That he especially had needs, needs that had not been tended to in a long, long time. He couldn't understand why she just didn't snap back. He had seen her come down stairs and act almost normal, although she was so frail and white and fragile looking. Her eyes drawn back in the sunken sockets of her skull, glassy and hollow. Talking, but not even hearing herself or knowing what she was saying. The last time he had hugged her she felt like a bundle of twigs dried from the sun and brittle enough to snap with his fingers. He felt bad for yelling at her when he realized that she couldn't help the way she was. He knew what it was like to be yelled at, and he didn't like the way it felt. At times it seemed like he was mad at the whole world. Bitterness seemed to fester in him like a little thorn stuck just beneath the skin. Close enough to see but still too deep for a needle. All you can do is prick it every once in a while to let the fever out and wait for it to work its way to the surface. Fever ran deep in Rube. So hot and deep and bitter that it would wake him up at night. Wake him up laying on sheets sweat through, his heart pounding on the back of his chest like a hard bass drum mallet slapping a tight leather head. He still loved her deeply. Though he was beginning to realize that that was becoming a lonely thing to do. She had held him many times during those nights. Held him to her chest and stroked his hair like a baby while he cried and cursed the demons that, after all those years, still chased him through his dreams and into her arms.

He had walked out onto the porch to clean the frame of the revolver. The fresh scent of linseed oil hung in the night air as he rubbed a rag across the little patches on its sides. The bluing had rubbed off from the friction of sliding it countless times in and out of the leather holster and would rust if left unoiled. He did not want to be seen all over town dragging around an old rusted revolver, nor did he want to spend the money on a new one. He had never really planned on being anybody's sheriff in the first place and he considered it a real nice coincidence that he just happened to own a good revolver and a holster that he hadn't had to pay for.

Rube sat and smoked as he stared out across the yard at the bare wire of the clothesline. He knew that there were chores still left to be done and he breathed deep at the thought of them. He knew the pain of loss and the need for time to grieve, and he had come to know that he needed Esther. He missed her and would be glad when she returned.

## COFFIN PINE

"WELL WHAT'S IT GONNA BE today, hun?" Darlene said as she stepped through the doors and set the coffee out in front of him. "Don't think we got any mince today but the peach sure looks good."

"Well, I tell you what sweetheart, I b'lieve I'm gonna have two eggs sunny side up and some of that ham and how 'bout biscuits?"

"You gonna skin my tail but I was runnin late this mornin' and I haven't had the time to make any biscuits. Oh I know you gonna kill me," she shrugged her shoulders and batted her eyelashes.

"Toast'll do fine," Rube said as he pulled out the little pouch and rolled a cigarette.

Darlene disappeared behind the doors and came back a few minutes later carrying hot coffee and slopped it into his cup.

"Didn't you get any breakfast at home?" she said as she leaned and rested on the counter.

"Naw, guess you didn't hear."

"Naw guess I didn't. What?"

"Esther walked out the other evenin' and PV was layin' out there in the stall next to that mule of his. That new buckskin. Both of 'em dead as coffin pine." He stuck the cigarette in his mouth and lit it and pulled the heat slowly up the paper and into his lungs.

"No she didn't," Darlene said, surprised.

"She did. I told her to go ahead and take a little time. We went over there the other night and she was real shook up about it. Ya know, I'd've never thought anybody'd get upset enough over a mule dyin to just up and die hisself," Rube stared into his coffee as he talked.

"Well whatta you think happen? I mean were they both just dead?"

"Yeah, Esther said she just walked out there and found both of 'em just layin there. I guess he went out there and found that mule and his heart just give out I s'pose. I never woulda thought anybody'd get that upset over a mule dyin'."

Guppy stood from a table in the corner of the room and walked toward the counter. Rube hadn't noticed him when he walked in and he flinched when Guppy slapped him on the back and sat down on the stool beside him.

"Why don't you go on back over yonder and mind your own damn business," Darlene snapped, waving her hand toward the back of the room.

"Why don't you shut the hell up and get me some of that there coffee," Guppy sneered back at her.

"Orville, you watch your mouth in here. Don't be startin' no trouble you hear me, or I'll take you over to the jail for disturbing the peace. You hear me now?" Rube set his cigarette in the ashtray and turned to face Guppy. He had known him to be very unpredictable and if he was going to try something Rube wanted to see it coming.

"Oh, now, I didn't mean nothin'. I's just talkin'. Could I please have some more coffee if it's not too much trouble dear." He grinned at Darlene as she took his cup and disappeared again behind the doors.

"Say old PV and his old mules just up and dropped dead, huh? I'll be damned. I cain't b'lieve that, couldn't help but overhear."

Rube turned back to face the counter and sipped at his coffee without answering.

"I'll be. What the hell happen? Them old mules just up and die on eem? Somebody kill 'em ? Poison't 'em or sumpin' ?"

"Just the buckskin," Rube sipped at his coffee without looking at Guppy.

"Well shit. Don't that just beat all to hell," Guppy laughed, "B'lieve that's the damnedest thing I ever heard. Somebody really poisoned 'em?"

"You seem to know a awful lot about it. Why don't you tell me what happened?" Rube turned his stool and looked at Guppy.

"Whatta you mean, 'tell you'. I's just talkin. I ain't got no idea what happen to that old nigger and his mules. This the first I heard anything 'bout it. I's just guessin' is all."

"Well you sure a good guesser."

"Well, don't look at me, I ain't did a damn thing. Cain't say as I wouldn't like to shake the hand of the sumbitch that did though. He got a bay too ain't he?" Guppy said.

"Still does. You wantin' a mule alluva sudden?"

"Aw hell, I ain't no farmer and even if I was I wouldn't have no mule that I'd get offa no nigger anyhow. Tell you that right now. I's justa wonderin' why whoever done it didn't finish the job that's all."

"Well I'll tell you what, why don't you pick yourself up and drag your no count sorry ass on outta here," Rube said, staring at Guppy.

Darlene walked back out and sat the cup in front of Guppy.

"Your service is too slow. I gotta be on my

way."

"Well now I gotta say, that just breaks my heart. You ain't gonna drink some of yer coffee 'fore ya go?" Darlene said, sliding the cup across the counter toward him.

"Nigger lover," Guppy mouthed under his breath as he stood and made his way across to the door and pulled it open and turned back to glare at Rube before slamming the door shut, the little bells jingling behind him.

"I hocked a good one in his coffee, shame I couldn't get eem to drink it. I wish he was the one that'd just dropped over dead," Darlene said, sloshing more coffee into Rube's cup.

"He keeps goin' on like he is and that may be just what he does one day."

VISIT

RUBE PULLED UP TO THE YARD and stopped before the front tires touched the grass. The house was open and still and he could see through the screen and kitchen and into the back yard. Esther had not heard him pull up and she was startled as he rounded the corner and called her name.

"Esther."

"Good Lord Sheriff, I didn't hear you pull in. Whew," she said, putting her hand over her chest.

"I didn't mean to scare ya," Rube said with a smile.

"Well what brings you out here this afternoon? Is everything alright ?" She looked concerned as she stepped toward him.

"Oh yes, yes. Everything' s alright. I just come by for a visit. Thought I'd see how you were gettin along that's all."

"Oh. Well that's sure thoughtful of you, Sheriff. I s'pose I'm doin' just fine. I can come back to work soon as you need me too."

"Well you just take your time. We'll make do 'til you get back. Wouldn't hurt me to lose a few inches around the waist anyhow." He tugged on his belt and grinned.

"The boys gettin' along okay?"

"Oh yeah, they're alright. Arliss was fussin' this mornin' 'bout breakfast though. Sayin' he'll sure be glad when you come back. Said his eggs were crunchy again. I never could crack those things without gettin' some of the shell in 'em."

"I tell you that boy is somethin' else." Esther laughed.

"He sure is. Say Esther, you know how bad we all feel about PV and all. I mean I just feel terrible for ya."

"Well I sure thank you, Sheriff. I sure do."

"Did they say for sure what it was that happened to him?"

"Said his heart just give out on eem was all. His heart hadn't been too good for some time."

"I didn't have no idea that he had a bad heart. Who'd've known it to look at eem. I just never would've thought that somebody'd get that upset over a mule dyin'."

"I s'pose he did. He sure had a lotta big ideas 'bout what he was gonna do with them mules. I s'pose it was just more than his old heart could take, goin out there and findin' her dead so sudden like he did."

"Well, I tell ya, you sure wouldn't've known he had a weak heart to look at eem, that's for sure. And who'd've thought somebody'd get that upset over a old mule dyin'."

"Well Sheriff, I guess he just had some big ideas about them mules," Esther said, hanging her head and looking at the ground.

"Well I'm sure nobody meant any harm to come to PV. I cain't say that I remember him ever doin wrong by anybody. Can you?"

"Nosuh, I don't guess I can at that."

Rube walked to the edge of the pen and leaned against a post and Esther followed along behind him.

"Is somethin wrong, Sheriff?"

"Oh no, Esther. I's just pokin' around is all."

"Yessuh."

"That other mule seems to be just fine don't he?" Rube said, pointing to Jack.

"Well now I don't know too awful much 'bout mules, but far as I can tell he seems to be just fine."

"Well I'm sure glad to hear that."

Rube stepped on the wire and pulled the fence open and climbed through into the pen, arching and twisting his back away from the little sharp barbs. Jack laid his ears back and stepped to the far side and turned and glared at him. He stopped and looked down at the thick scrape in the dirt where Rosie had been dragged across the pen and down the road. He felt a stirring in the pit of his stomach and he closed his eyes and shook his head. The shade thrown from the lean-to felt cool and he patted at his cheeks with the sleeve of his shirt as he stepped around the small dung piles to the trough and ran his hand along the metal.

"Good Lord," he mouthed under his breath.

"Well I don't wanna keep you Esther, I just thought I'd stop by."

"Well that sure is kind of you, Sheriff. I sure do thank you."

"You just come on back soon as you can, alright. You know, soon as you feel up to it. We'll make do 'til then," Rube reached and patted her on the arm and walked back to the car and pulled out of the drive.

Esther stood in the front yard and watched as he drove away. It was a curious visit and she stood there watching until the car was completely gone.

## DEAR COMPANION

I THINK MAYBE IT'S THE stillness that gets to me the most. I don't guess I can remember a time ever in my life that things was so quiet. I was just still a baby when my babies popped out hollerin' and screamin' and kickin'. I used to think they weren't never gonna stop screamin'. Bet they still screamin' right now. I lay here sometimes and it gets so quiet I swear I can hear the grass and the weeds and kudzu growin' outside. Hear it right through the walls. Growin' all up the sides of the house. Sometimes I hear PV callin' to me right from the grave. So still and quiet I can hear eem sayin' my name right down the hall. Makes me start thinkin' I'm goin crazy. Losin' my mind. Layin' here wide-eyed listenin' to all that quiet. I always thought I'd be the first one to die. Oh yeah, he was older than me, but I still thought I'd go first. I used to think about it. I'd wonder what he'd do without me. The thought of him needin' me so much and missin' me so much that he'd just sit down and cry. Used to make me feel good inside. I'd smile when I'd picture eem tryin' to do all the things I do 'round here. Me just sittin' up there on a cloud lookin' down on eem. Him down there scrubbin' holes in all his clothes and burnin' up everything he try to cook, cryin' and nearly starvin' hisself to death. I'd laugh out loud sometimes and he'd just look at me and shake his head like he had any idea what I was thinkin'. I never thought about what I'd do if he went on before me. Never thought about that at all. I's so sure it would be the other way around. I wish I had thought some about it now. Like all his things. They still just layin' all around here. He's got fresh shirts hangin' in the closet. I had just done 'em and put 'em up without so much as thinkin' about it. Even pressed 'em out a little 'fore I caught myself. I see 'em in there hangin' and I don't know what I'm s'posed to do with 'em. I cain't wear 'em. I don't wanna just throw 'em out and they too nice still to just make rags out of 'em or sumpin' like that but I don't guess I really want 'em to just hang in there forever for me to have to look at every day. He's got boots and hats and things strewn all over this house from one end to the other. I used to say, "Lord PV, you just like a freight train runnin' through the front door." Used to fuss at eem all the time to pick up. He'd just laugh. That laugh. Loud and big. It'd fill up this whole house and echo around for what seemed like days at a time. I never noticed how dark this old place is. Never noticed that before. Even with the windows open in the middle of the afternoon, it's still dark. Funny how I never noticed that before. There's still a pair of his coveralls layin all crumpled up in the corner. Right over there in the corner. I just haven't been able to pick them up. Been layin' there a while I guess. I'd have picked them up right quick before. Lookin' back guess I fussed at him a lot about that. Don't seem to bother me so much now.

Ya know, I cried when they drug Rosie off. Sat down and cried just like a baby. The reverend and four other men came from the church and wrapped a chain around her hind legs and drug her off up the road. S'pose they burned her. Too big to bury. Watchin' that old mule drag up the road made me feel like I'd been kicked in the stomach. Just kicked right in the stomach with somebody's old boot. If I had to guess, I'd say PV's got quite a good laugh outta that. Watchin' me cry over that old mule. Yeah I s'pect he got quite a laugh. I guess it's the quiet that gets to me the most. The stillness. I just never thought it'd be so quiet.

## FINISH THE JOB

GUPPY STOPPED JUST INSIDE THE door and adjusted his eyes in the smoky darkness. The laughing faces distorted in the drifting smoke, moved syrupy and ghostlike in the dizziness of his brain. He staggered across the room and slid on to a stool at the bar.

"You heard about that damned nigger and his mules," the words barely audible through his dry, thick tongue.

No one acknowledged him as he looked around the room and fumbled about his shirt for a cigarette.

"Damn nigger. Ain't such a big shot now is he?"

"All day long. Nigger just walkin' 'long, mule ass prancin' around dirty sonuvabitch, the bitches. He think he just gonna come in here and smartass around and think nobody ain't gonna put a stop to it, well somebody sure put a stop to it alright. I tell you right now, God don't like it. Don't like it one little bit. Hey you listenin'? Hey gimme a beer. Hey." Guppy laid stretched across his arm on the bar.

"Sit up and stop slobberin' on that bar," the bartender said as he slapped a damp towel across Guppy's face, "Sit up I said. I just about had it with your sorry ass."

"Hey don't slap, old dishrag, gimme a beer."

Guppy was long past the point of being able to make much sense but he was able to dig in his pocket and drop some change out in front of him. The bartender raked the change off in his hand and sat a bottle up on the bar.

"This the only one you gonna get so drink it down and get on outta here. I need business but you startin' to make me wonder just how bad." He turned and walked to the end of the bar and wiped at it with the rag.

Guppy took the bottle and spun around to face the room. His lips mouthed as he ranted between gulps and his rank and senseless babble fell silent as it mingled in with the laughter and senseless babble of the others in the room. He waved his hand as he rambled and shifted his eyes from one shapeless face to another, unaware that his preaching fell on deaf ears. He finished the beer and set it on the bar and stood and stared at the bartender who was still standing at the end of the bar. The bartender laughed to himself as Guppy cussed him and walked out the door.

"Hey, couldn't help but overhear ya in there."

Sonny and three others slid alongside and in behind Guppy as he stumbled out on to the sidewalk. They had been hanging around the front door trying, with no apparent luck, to get their hands on some beer when Guppy stepped outside.

Guppy looked cross-eyed through the haze at the boys but didn't say anything.

"Damn shame, ain't it?" Sonny said.

"What?" Guppy slurred softly.

"Damn niggers is what. Thinkin' they can come in here and just take over." Sonny looked back at the boys walking behind Guppy and smiled and winked. One of the boys held his hand over his mouth to keep from laughing out loud.

Guppy stopped and straightened himself, "Hell yes, it is," he yelled out. "Shame. Daddy lived here and never did have to tol'rate it. You know. Shame. Niggers. Damn niggers!"

The boy who had covered his mouth now lagged behind the others and turned his back on them and laughed out loud before skipping back up to join the group.

"Damn niggers is right and somebody oughta do somethin' 'bout it, I tell you that right now. One dead nigger and one dead nigger mule ain't gonna get it done."

Sonny reached up and put his arm around Guppy's shoulder and motioned to the boy who had now stopped laughing.

As Sonny patted Guppy on the shoulder and the back, the boy rifled the loose pocket of Guppy's pants and slid out his wallet. As they walked along he opened it and took out three moist paper bills, folded it closed and slid it back into the pocket.

"Damn right they oughta. Teach 'em a lesson once and for all. Finish the job. Damn smart boys you boys. Finish the job."

"Damn smart is right. Smart enough to know they oughta do somethin' 'bout stinkin' old drunks walkin' 'round town, too, that's what they really oughta do somethin' about." Sonny took his arm from around Guppy's shoulder and sneered at him.

"What?!" Guppy yelled.

"You heard me, you sorry drunk."

"W'y I teach you some respect you little bastards I'll finish the..."

Sonny reached and pushed him as hard as he could. Guppy lost his balance and slammed on to the ground and laid still staring up at the sky.

"Hell Sonny, you don't think you kill't eem do ya?", one of the other boys asked, looking down at Guppy and snickering.

"Aw to hell with him. I didn't hurt eem. He's just drunk is all. Let's get outta here 'fore somebody comes along. He can lay right there 'til Jesus comes back for all I care."

Guppy laid there without moving and listened to the shuffling feet fade in the night. He stared up at the sky and watched the stars and the clouds and wondered if he might just sling off of this whirling, spinning earth out into space and crash hard against the moon and dig his face into its cheesy surface and eat his way through to the other side.

AND THEY CRIED WITH A LOUD VOICE saying How long O Lord holy and true dost though not judge and avenge our blood on them that dwell on the earth? And white robes were given unto every one of them and it was said unto them that they should rest yet for a little season until their fellowservants also and their brethren that should be killed as they were should be fulfilled. And I beheld when he had opened the sixth seal and lo there was a great earthquake and the sun became black as sackcloth of hair and the moon became as blood and the stars of heaven fell unto earth even as a fig tree casteth her untimely figs when she is shaken of a mighty wind. And heaven departed as a scroll when it is rolled together and every mountain and island were moved out of their places. And the kings of the earth and the great men and the rich men and the chief captains and the mighty men and every bondman and every free man hid themselves in the dens and in the rocks of the mountains; and said to the mountains and rocks, fall on us and hide us from the face of him that sitteth on the throne and from the wrath of the lamb: For the great day of his wrath is come: and who shall be able to stand?

REVELATION 6: 10-17

SHE WOKE IN THE STICKY PITCH that hung in the room and lay frozen and wide-eyed as she listened to the bellowing of the anxious mule. The floor cold beneath her feet as she swung her legs off the side of the bed and stood and shuffled sluggish to the window. Jack's head arched to the stars, he neighed and pranced in the pen and as she turned back to her bed she saw the movement flash between the planks of the lean-to.

A deep grunt expelled from him and his body jerked hard at the clicking that popped out from behind and echoed in the stall. He wheeled around to face her, his chest heaving and forcing his hot breath into the air around him, flushing his face.

Guppy raised his hand and pointed the bony fingers at Esther.

"Let me tell you how things work 'round here, Nigger." His lips snarled revealing the yellowish brown teeth encased in the black outline of tobacco-stained gums as he took two small steps toward her.

The hammer clicked as it fell and slammed on to the primer cap of the paper shell. The left barrel rang out, pounding and vibrating the ground like a thunderclap as it exploded, expelling a flash of brilliant orange flame, cotton wadding and round lead pellets out the 16 gauge opening at its end. The heel of the stock jumped and bucked violently from the recoil causing her to have to shuffle her feet to keep herself from losing her balance. She closed her eyes and shook her head in sharp little jerks as if affected by a sudden chill. The ringing in her ears made her dizzy and she opened her eyes to see Jack backed all the way into the lean-to, pushing his haunches against the rough planks, his ears laid back on his neck and his front hooves stomping at the hard, packed clay. Esther pressed her face into the bend of her right arm and wiped the sleeve hard against her brow as the barrels of the shotgun dropped with a dull thud on to the ground at her feet. She breathed the fresh smell of the fabric deep into her lungs and thought of PV and how she would hug him in the mornings after he would dress and how he would smell in the clean cotton shirts as she pressed the side of her face against his chest. She wished he were here. She wished she were with him. She wished she had never gone out of the house. To hell with Jack, she thought. Son of a bitch never gave PV nothin' but trouble anyhow. What was he thinkin', tryin' all this nonsense about making a living off of cotton. It ain't been nothin' but a struggle to get anything to grow. Crazy fool like to killed himself trying to get them sweet potatoes and peanuts to come up. He just had to set his sights on being a cotton farmer. Now look where that had gotten both of them. For the first time in her life she really wished, for a moment more than anything else, that she were white. Just an ordinary white farmer's wife. She wished PV were white. Nobody important, just white. Just two people that blended in. Two people that nobody paid much attention to. She felt ashamed for it. Shame on her father and mother whom she loved so much. But she couldn't help it, she felt it all the same. If she were a white woman and a black man had come up on her place she would be expected to do exactly what she did. Nobody would give a damn. She wanted it all to be a dream. Just another bad dream like she had as a child. She felt the tears stream down her cheeks and she wiped the sleeve across her eyes and lifted her face and gazed at the far side of the pen. She began to inch her way across, dragging the shotgun on the ground, the barrels scratching and scoring the clay with the little silver bead sight that stuck perched atop the blued steel.

A contorted mass entangled in rusty barbs and braided wire lay quiet and motionless in the darkness in front of her. The gaunt arms fully outstretched as if restrained, impaled in some invisible crucifixion. Guppy's head lay back, dangling over the top wire. Specks of blood splattered about his cheeks and chin and neck. His mouth agape, his eyes wide open, fixed in a blank stare up at the black sky like a freckle-faced, awestruck kid scanning the constellations in search of the Big Dipper. The once white cotton shirt now soaked with a mixture of bile and blood, black and sticky like warm tar in the moonlight as it dripped and pooled on the ground beside him. The flesh of his stomach lay open. Peeled back. Esther turned and felt the involuntary jerk in the pit of her stomach, the burning in her throat. She leaned forward and vomited hard on to the ground. She caught her breath and wiped at her mouth and then jerked forward again. The rancid smell filled the lean-to and she heaved and coughed again before catching her breath and staggered to the trough and knelt down and cupped her hands and splashed the cool water on to her face and into her mouth. She rinsed and spit and wiped her face on her dress and sat down and leaned her back against the trough and cried.

## KEROSENE

ESTHER SAT UP AND LOOKED across the pen. She was no longer crying as she stared at the tattered carcass. She paced back and forth in front of him and lectured as though she were scolding a schoolboy.

"Just couldn't leave it alone could ya? No not you. Wudn't good enough fo' ya to get my PV and Rosie. Nosuh, not you. You just got to come back and get old wore out Jack. Yeah, and me too from the looks of it. They gonna string me up fo sho over this mess. They gonna string me up fo' sho. You a evil- doin' sonuvabitch, that's what you are. You a evil-doin' sonuvabitch. Not no more though. You ain't gonna be doin' no evil no more that's fo' sho, we done seen to that now ain't we and I tell you what, you ain't gonna get me. Nosuh, you ain't gonna get me. Tell me how things work 'round here, huh. Well looks like I'm the one did all the tellin'." Her arms crossed tight against her body as she ranted and raved like a lunatic caught in the snares of dementia.

She looked across the pen once more wishing that the body would be gone and that she could realize that it was all a dream, but it wasn't gone and she knew that it would be there tomorrow and the day after and the day after that. Just lying there in the sun for anybody that might just happen by to see. Lying there until she took it off. She wanted to get Sheriff Whitlock. She wanted to believe that she meant enough to him and the boys that he would help her but she knew better. He seemed to be a decent enough white man but he was just that. A white man and she was a black woman that had just blown the guts out of another white man. Like it or not, Sheriff Whitlock never would get away with protecting a black over a white, even if she did make the best biscuits and gravy that he had ever ate. They'd expect him to do something about all this and they probably wouldn't settle for anything short of seeing her hanging from a tree on the courthouse lawn. She remembered how just a while back he'd talked about somebody beating up a black boy over at Lutie like it was just something to pass the time. He even kind of chuckled when he said that whoever done it kicked that boy in the balls until they almost swelled up and burst. She wanted to pray, but she was so mad at the Lord that she didn't even want to talk to him much less pray and wait until he got around to answering her.

She walked back over to the carcass and nudged the bottom of Guppy's boot. She stared into his eyes and wished that she had left the shotgun in the closet and just pulled the quilt back over her head when she had heard Jack bray. If she had never gone out to check on him, none of this would have happened. She'd have woken up in the morning and Jack would have been dead and that would have been just fine with her. Just one less headache to worry about. She'd never cared about mules anyway. They ain't as pretty as a horse and they're damn near too stubborn to ride. She gazed out through the darkness and scanned the treeline and as far into the field as she could see and thought again about the boy that had been beaten. She could almost see him in her mind. The pain he must have felt when the boots smashed into his groin. The fear and shame and embarrassment of sitting in that sheriff's office lying about what had happened. Playing the fool who'd busted his own balls. She laughed as she remembered the time PV had busted his balls trying to step across a fence and how he had sat on the porch for two days saying it hurt too much to walk so he'd just sit. The thought of those white boys kicking and laughing and kicking that boy made her want to cry, and it made her mad at the man that lay in front of her. Mad at him for trying to do to her just what those boys had done. Kick somebody when they're down. She remembered the big cottonwood that stood lifeless deep in the pasture beside the road that led from her house to town. The black branches running varicose up and out of the thick arterial trunk into the creamy clouds of the morning sky creaking and popping and straining in the breeze as it rustled through them. Long wounds where the coarse bark had rotted and flaked away like burned flesh falling off of bone, exposing the grayish white wood beneath, peppered with worm holes, its marrow dried and regurgitated pulp. She had watched through her window and seen the faint orange glows that flickered all around its base. She had seen in the mornings after, the limbs twisting against the sky up and out of the top of the hill like snakes. She knew what happened there in the night and she had felt the skin crawl along her spine as she inched past and tried not to look.

Esther turned back to the corpse and nudged Guppy's boot once more with her toe, then turned and climbed through the barbed wire and scurried back across to the house. Jack could see her dark silhouette passing back and forth behind the window and she soon stepped back outside and scurried over to the pen. In her arms she carried a wad of sheets, a little rectangle shaped cardboard box, a claw hammer and a small tin jug with a short spout sticking out of its top. She dropped one of the sheets on the ground and smoothed out it's edges with her foot and sat the tin jug and the remaining sheets in its center. She then disappeared into the darkness of the stall and fumbled around clumsily. Jack, still nervous from the scent of death, stayed on the far side of the pen and watched as she stepped back out and dropped the contents of her arms on to the sheet. She stepped back into the stall and took a short lead line and a long rope that hung neatly coiled from a nail on the back wall. A little tin can, rusted and without a label, sat on a board in the stall and she reached her fingers into it and took a small handful of nails and dropped them down into the pocket on the front of her dress and walked to the trough where she dropped the rope in the cool green water and turned to look at Jack and then again at the corpse.

"Ho there Jack boy, ho now," she said as she inched toward him.

"We got a little work to do, me and you. Now I cain't get it done without ya, so you just keep still now."

Jack jerked his head as the lead line snapped into the ring under his halter and he danced from side to side as she led him across the pen and tied the line to the fence next to the Guppy's body. He was heavier than she thought he would be, and when she sat him up and got behind and wrapped her arms around his waist to lift him, her hand slid into the open wound. The warm, moist jelly of his organs squished between her fingers. She screamed out as she jerked her hand back and wiped it on his shirt. Her stomach jerked up a hard gag but she pushed it down and when she reached around again she was careful to raise her hands up to his chest. She lifted him until she was on her knees and as she lunged upright, his head bobbed backward and the heavy base of his skull hit her square on the end of the nose. She closed her eyes and felt the tears well up as blood dripped from her left nostril and mixed with the greasy hair that hung from the back of his head and mopped across her face. In frustration she popped him forward, slinging his head down and bouncing his chin off of his chest. His feet turned inward and his legs folded as if the fabric tubes of his pants were empty and dangling on a clothesline as she dragged him toward Jack. Jack jumped hard to the side as Esther propped Guppy up against him and she stumbled almost letting the limp corpse fall. When Jack jumped he had jumped toward the fence and he was now wedged between the sharp barbs and the carcass. He eased himself away from the fence and into the softness of the man as Esther paused to catch her breath before grabbing Guppy around the bottom of his legs. She lifted him until he draped across the middle of Jack's swayed back. He stood still as Esther walked back across the pen and took the hammer from the middle of the sheet. She went to the side of the stall and pried two plank boards off its wall. After she dropped the hammer back on the sheet, she folded the corners and tied it into a knapsack then took the soaked rope from the trough and slid her arm through it until it hung in the joint of her shoulder. She took the knapsack and the two boards and grabbed the lead rope and led Jack out across the field, stopping now and then to push on the belt and slide the body to balance again across the mule's back. She inched along all but invisible in the darkness until she and Jack and Guppy were swallowed whole by the black treeline.

She crept, darting back and forth, jutting her face out at the darkness and squinting her eyes at the swaying outlines that moved in succession with the clouds blowing across the tree tops strobing silver beams through the intricate patterns of leafy webs that fused together above her head. She froze and pitched her head to the side and listened as the wind brushed across the ground, lifting and dropping and lifting again, the thicket floor. A pulsating, breathing carpet that swirled and rustled around her feet. She stood stock-still and pressed her cheek against the rubbery muscle of the mule's jaw with the lead rope pulled taut to the ground, surveyed her position and turned, changing her course to a more westward approach before setting off again tugging and cussing Jack. Esther moved along with carefully placed steps, squinting and panting and fanning at the darkness until about a hundred yards in front of her she could see the trunks begin to thin, and the deep purple of the night seeping in between the shadows of the dense thicket. She crossed half the distance, tied the mule to a sapling, inched her way to the edge of the trees and crouched on her haunches in the weeds and grass that filled the overgrown ditch running alongside the road. A queasy stir churned in the pit of her stomach as she looked out through the rusty barbs across the pasture at the hill. Two tiny yellow dots appeared on the back side of the pasture and made a soft steady whine as they grew and lit the gravel and dust that stirred under and in front and all around them. Esther had not noticed the truck until it was almost right on top of her and she pitched forward and fell flat on her stomach and held her breath as it rolled by followed by two tiny red dots burning down past her like two spent matches. The night once again became still. She stood up in the ditch, brushed at her clothes and walked back to the sapling and pulled the lead rope until Jack stomped after her. Once she stepped into the open, she pulled hard and the mule hopped across the ditch and stepped clumsily up on to the road. Esther crossed and stepped into the ditch on the other side as Jack crossed behind her and stopped abruptly with both hooves dug into the dirt on the top edge of the ditch. He neighed as he pulled against the line and she cussed him and jerked at the halter.

"Gitcho no count ass down here, Lord!" Esther pulled.

Jack didn't budge as she yanked on the line. She let the rope slack in her hand, then snapped her wrist up and popped the rope against the underside of his chin. Jack brayed out and tried to rear up but Esther jerked down hard again on the rope digging the halter into his face.

"You gonna go across this ditch, if you got to do it over my dead body." She talked to Jack, but mostly to herself, as she turned and stepped up out of the ditch and on to the road and stood next to him.

The dull thud of the hammer popped off his flank as Esther slung the knapsack as hard as she could directly across the ass of the stubborn mule. Jack yelled at the shock and bounced as he went into the ditch and jumped through the high grass and weeds and stood breathing heavy, waiting for Esther. The limp and dripping load on his back draped heavy to one side and he could feel it sliding toward the ground. Esther stepped down and waded across the ditch. She grabbed the back of Guppy's shirt and pushed him back into position, took the lead rope and pulled Jack across the sagging fence and through the pasture toward the little hill. Tears dripped from her eyes as she stood atop the crest and peered down. It looked the way it always had with the limbs scraggly and brittle and bare and she felt the chills run up and down her arms and the middle of her spine as she eased her way down. She pulled on the lead line until Jack was standing just beneath the tree and she dropped the knapsack on the ground beside him. Some of the kerosene had sloshed out of it's can and soaked the fabric and she tore it into small strips and took the strips and tucked them into Guppy's pants pockets. The grass braids felt cool and heavy, and the water ran down her hands as she tied the waterlogged rope around the base of the tree and threw it over the limb and tied the other end around Guppy's neck. Jack flinched as the thin oily liquid saturated the hair and clothes and skin of the load that lay draped across his back. Esther took the last of the strips of cloth and held it to the opening of the tin and drenched it with the fuel. She lifted Guppy's head and forced the rag deep into his mouth leaving a piece to hang out just past the lips like a fuse.

The planks were dry and brittle and she laid them out carefully on the ground, one across the other, and drove four nails into the intersection where the two crossed. The nails were long and they sank into the planks and drove through both boards and she scratched her forearm as she raised the cross and laid it back to rest propped against the tree. She leaned back against the tree and held her arm and cried as she stared into Guppy's dead eyes.

"You a evil-doin' sonuvabitch." Esther wiped at her eyes and stepped toward the mule.

"Sweet Jesus, help me."

She pulled on the line and eased Jack out from under the tree.

Jack felt the load slide down his back and off his rump and he heard the creaking and popping as the full weight of the lifeless man swung below the limb. Esther walked back to Guppy and took hold of his pant leg and stopped him from swinging. The vapors strong in her nostrils as she scratched the match across the cardboard box and touched it to the short fuse that dangled from Guppy's lips. She could see the flame explode in his mouth and the flesh on his cheeks begin to melt away as the fire jumped from the fuse down on to his shirt and pants. He was completely engulfed in the bright orange heat almost before she could step clear. It surprised her how fast he had burned, and she stood and stared into the heat before turning back toward Jack. She placed the hammer and tin jug back in the center of the sheet and folded it back into the knapsack. She grabbed a large wad of mane and slung herself up on to the back of the mule and reached down and took up the lead line and kicked Jack in his flank as hard as she could. Jack broke into a trot back up the little hill and crossed the pasture. Esther pulled him up and looked as far as she could see in both directions and kicked him again until he had stepped through the overgrown ditch and back across the road. She turned and saw the night sky painted with the faint orange glow and she kicked Jack hard and they disappeared back into the black treeline.

MAGGIE

MAGGIE WELLS STUNK WHEN SHE talked, and she talked almost all the time. The smell of her breath and her body swirled in the tepid air as she stepped into the little office and sat down. She admired the deep gouges that ran against, across and with the grain; cutting delicate patterns across the rich mahogany desk that stood in front of her. She parted her legs at the knees, leaned forward and rested her elbows on her meatless thighs and pulled her upper arms into her torso, squeezing her breasts together, as the footsteps grew louder behind her.

"Sit up there, Maggie. I can see your tits hangin' down like a old bitch dog," Rube said as he walked around the desk and slid into his chair. He had known her ever since he could remember and would not deny that at one time, a long time before the wear of childbirth, grain liquor, bad love and Lord only knows what else had gotten a hold of her, she had not been so bad to look at.

She grinned as she sat back in the chair.

"That sonuvabitch has run off. You seen eem around?"

"Hold on a minute, what son of a bitch?"

Maggie sat staring at Rube without saying anything.

"You talkin 'bout Guppy?"

"You know damn good and well who I'm talkin about Rubal. I cain't find eem nowheres and I ain't found nobody that's seen eem in over a week and we s'pose to get married."

"Married," Rube leaned forward and grinned at Maggie. "Why in hell would you wanna go and do a thing like that?"

"Now either you bein' a smartass or you just 'bout the dumbest sheriff I'd ever know." She looked down and picked at her finger nails as she talked.

"You in the family way again! Good Lord Maggie, we gonna have to lock that thing up." Rube laughed and slapped the top of his desk.

"It ain't funny, you sonuvabitch, it ain't funny at all. He oughtn't to be able to just up and run off. He oughtn't to. They oughta be some kinda law against it." The light-hearted smile had drawn from her face and she looked distant. Defeated and desperate. Immune to the defiance with which she once faced the world.

"How do you know that it's his?"

She glared across the desk and Rube knew that that was a line of questioning that did not need to be followed any further. Everyone knew about Maggie and Guppy, and her look was enough answer for him.

"I mean have you told him about it?" Rube already knew she had, but asked anyway out of uncomfortable awkwardness.

"Hell, yes, I told him. Why you think he just up and disappeared? He ain't nothin' but a no count sorry bastard and you need to get up offa your lazy ass and go hunt him down and make him git back here and marry me like he said he was!" Maggie's upper lip trembled as she talked and she looked like she was about to cry.

Rube saw the tears welling in her eyes and he stood up and sat on the corner of his desk.

"Now listen Maggie, I'll go on out there to his house this afternoon and see if I cain't find eem. But now I cain't make nobody marry nobody and if'n he did in fact just up and run off there ain't a whole lot that I can do about that. They ain't no law that says a man cain't just pick up and leave. I ain't got much to say 'bout old Guppy sep for the fact that you and that youngun might both be better off if'n he did just up and run off. Seems to me like you ain't seen nothin but trouble ever since you took up with him anyhow."

"Who asked you anything about that, Rubal? I never come in here to ask you nothin 'bout what you think about it. Just see if you cain't find eem somewheres. Okay?" she reached up and wiped the tear from her face as it ran down her cheek.

"Awright Maggie, you know I will," Rube reached down and patted her shoulder, "go on home and I'll let you know."

Maggie stood and pulled the front top of her dress up to her face and wiped at her eyes again. The skin stretched taut over the bones in her arms and hands. A paunch bubbled out from beneath the midsection of her dress between the two sharp points of her hip bones as she stood and tugged at the dress until it twisted itself back into place. She seemed unaware of the looks that followed her as she stepped from the office and made her way out on to the street. Her skin and pores spongy and saturated with alcohol that seeped in the afternoon sun and bubbled up around her upper lip and forehead and trickled down her temple in a diluted salty mixture. Her head pounded in the bright light as she turned and made her way up the street.

They speckled the room, hunched in the dark corners like gargoyles carved from gray stone, permanently bonded on perches behind claw-clasped goblets of amber liquid. Their movements were methodical and seemed to slow time as they nursed. Light shot through the opening, temporarily exposing the zombified faces that sat scattered about the tables. A low grumble resonated in the air as Maggie stepped through the door. Smoke hovered like storm clouds over a midnight graveyard. She saw herself in the mirror behind the bottles as her eyes adjusted to the darkness and she watched her slow metamorphosis in the familiarity and comfort of her surroundings.

The short balding bartender stepped from behind a heavy, red curtain that hung in a narrow doorway behind the bar. He was rubbing his hands on a towel tucked into the waistband of his pants when he looked up and saw her sitting there.

"Maggie Wells. I ain't seen you in some time. What brings you in to this fine establishment this afternoon?" He laughed at his own sarcasm as he walked toward her.

"I tell you one thing, it sure is hot out there. Damn hot for this time of the day." She reached and patted the sweat from around her lip and her forehead.

"You right about that. Too hot to be out walkin' 'round in it that's for sure."

"Wish you'd get ridda that stupid mirror back there. Don't know why nobody'd just wanna sit and stare at themselves anyway." She laughed awkwardly at the small talk.

"They say it makes the room look bigger. That's how come it to be there. Don't know if it does or not but that's how come it to be there."

"Well, guess I'll take somethin' cold to drink. Just whatever you got back there'll be fine." Her tone was matter of fact, and she looked out around the room and not at him as she placed her order.

The short bartender didn't say anything and he didn't move toward filling her order, he just held his hand out in front of him and waited for her to turn back and notice.

"Aw come on, Lou," she said as she turned and saw the open palm. "Don't be such a hardass. It's hot and I'm parched as I can be. Come on."

"You know I don't sell no drinks on credit Maggie. If I was to give everybody in town a drink ever time they got parched I'd be dry as driftwood in a day or two."

"You ain't got to give everybody a drink. Hell, I thought we was friends."

"Well now you gonna hurt my feelings, Maggie. Friends is friends and business is business. You know that. You got to pay. You just got to, and that's all there is to it." He smiled and winked at her.

She felt the heavy thud pound behind her temples as she spun the stool and looked out through the dim, musty room. No one moved. No one looked up. They just sat and stared vacantly into the darkness in front of them and sipped on the warm drinks that had once been cool. She leaned forward and squinted her eyes as she studied each face. Her eyes fixed on a figure toward the back of the room and she held her hand up over her eyes as if to shield them from the sun.

"Is that Bobby Billings yonder?" she asked the bartender. "Kinda looks like eem."

"Naw, That ain't him. I ain't never seen that fella."

She leaned forward and squinted hard again until she too was convinced that the figure was a stranger.

"Come on, Lou, just one drink and I'll go on."

She turned back around and faced him as she begged.

"Maggie, I'm sorry but I just cain't give no handouts."

"I hate you, you sonuvabitch," she said as she slid off the stool and walked around behind the bar.

The short, fat, balding bartender smiled as he pulled back the heavy red curtain and disappeared with Maggie into the little room. Within minutes the bartender reemerged from behind the curtain. The towel no longer tucked into the waistband of his pants and a deep pinkish hue tinting his round, doughy face. He breathed heavy as he filled one of the glass mugs and set it out on the bar. Maggie stepped from behind the curtain tugging on her dress and pushing her hands through the matted strands of hair that now hung tasseled and disheveled down her shoulders. The same pinkish hue tinted her drawn cheeks and she gnawed her upper lip as she shuffled back around to the barstool in front of the glass. Her hand trembled as she raised the mug and gulped at it until the beer was gone. She popped it back down in front of her and the bartender took it and filled it again and again.

## GOOD SIZE MESS

"WHAT'D OLD MAGGIE WANT, RUBE?" Boots asked as Rube stepped from the office.

"Oh she wants me to go out and look for Guppy. You know it's as if I ain't got nothin' better to do then to tend to his sorry old ass."

"Whatta ya mean look for eem? How come she cain't go look for eem?"

"Said she has been and cain't find eem. I don't know why in hell she'd wanna find him but she wants to." Rube shook his head both with disgust and sympathy.

"Seems like I saw eem just the other night, cain't now remember where it was. Does she think somethin's happen to eem or somethin'?"

"Naw, she just thinks he's run off from her. Says she's pregnant. Don't go around tellin' everybody that though. Hell, if she is pregnant by Guppy, she's got enough to worry about without everybody talkin'."

"Good Lord. She think it's his for sure?"

"There ain't no tellin' what she thinks. I guess she figures it might be. Guppy musta figured that too if he just up and ran off."

"Well I hate to say it, but that might be the smartest thing he ever done. Can you just imagine the mess we'd have around here if the two of them got married and started tryin' to raise a youngun? And then started havin' more younguns. Hell," Boots laughed and rubbed his forehead.

"To be real honest, I don't wanna imagine nothin' of the sort." Rube turned and walked toward the door. "I told her I'd go look for eem though. 'Tween me and you I ain't gonna look too hard. Far as I'm concerned, good riddance to that crazy old bastard."

"You really think he just run off ? I mean you don't think somethin' mighta happened to eem do ya?"

"I don't guess I got any idea," Rube said.

"Well, you know what I'm startin to think? I'm startin' to think he mighta done somethin' to that old mule of PV's. That's what I'm startin' to think. I mean somethin' happened to that mule to cause it to just drop dead. I mean somethin' had to've happen to that mule to cause her to just up and drop dead so sudden like she did. Don't you think, Rube?"

"Well what, you think Guppy poisoned that mule?" Rube stared at Boots.

"Well she was pretty old, I guess, but I find it a little hard to b'lieve that she just fell over dead. Don't you? Guppy's been rantin' and ravin' around about it ever since he found out."

"Well, somethin' happen to it alright. But who in the world woulda thought PV'd get so upset over it that he'd fall over dead right on top of her. I mean Lord, what a mess. Nobody'd ever think killin' a man's mule'd kill the damn man. Lord. " Rube looked at the floor as he talked.

"Yeah, it's a good size mess alright. Ya know they's plenty of people that'd wanna knock that fool's head off. Guppy, I mean. I don't know that one of 'em might notta done just that. He coulda just run off though. If he did poison that mule he mighta thought you'd try and do somethin' about it on accounta Esther and all and he mighta just picked up and left. I mean he don't seem to have much goin' for himself here."

"Yeah, that old place of his mama's shoulda been torn down years ago and if he thinks he's gonna have to find some kinda work so he can raise a youngun, well then, he might have gotten drunk enough to just disappear. Like I said, I don't really care where he is just as long as he stays there."

"Well I'll ask around too and see if anybody's seen eem."

"Well don't do too much askin' around. We don't need all this nonsense stirrin' up down here. I can think of at least five people off the top of my head who are glad to see that old mule dead and I can think of at least a dozen more who ain't losin' no sleep over the where abouts of Orville Walters. You know what I mean."

"Yeah, I know whatcha mean. I'm kinda like you. I don't really care where that sumbitch is long as he ain't around here wartin' us to death."

"I guess I'm gonna take a drive out by his place and see if maybe he's layin' in there drunk or dead or somethin'. I'll see ya later."

By the time Rube got back, Boots and everyone else had left. The door was locked and it was quiet. He stepped into his office and sat down behind his desk and rubbed his eyes with the palms of his hands. He sat for a long time in the silence. The emptiness around him calm and soothing as he sat there in the darkness. He thought of Maggie and Guppy and Esther and his sons and his wife and daughter. He thought about blacks and whites and the Klan and mules and farming and cotton and life and just the day-to-day living of it. He couldn't remember when life was anything other than a chore. Something that took a lot of effort and doing. Not just something you are but something you have to do. How in the hell was anybody supposed to know that PV had a weak heart? He had seen that old field full of sand and rock. PV could dig around out there with a hundred mules and still not have ground fit for nothing. Buying that old buckskin wasn't gonna do nothing except get him strung up. That was all he needed, a damn lynching right here before he could get re-elected. They just weren't gonna let it be. No way in hell they gonna have it around here. Just gonna keep stirring it and stirring it. That old man didn't deserve to get hurt. Not over a damn mule. Especially a mule that he didn't even really need anyhow. How in hell could anybody have known about PV's heart? Who'd know it to look at him. Lord what a mess.

He felt the heaviness bearing down on his shoulders and a dull thud begin to thump somewhere deep behind his eyes as he thought slow and deliberate and then he sat without thinking at all.

SLOWBURN

"GOOD LORD, BOOTS, CUT HIM outta there 'fore somebody comes along and sees eem, Jesus," Rube said as he stepped down the hill and walked toward the tree.

"Bo's on his way with the truck. Should be pullin' up any time. You didn't say anything 'bout this to anybody else did ya?"

"Naw. I thought I'd better wait for you to get here before I touched eem though. Maybe you oughta be the one to cut eem down."

"Like hell I oughta. You cut eem down and do it right now and I ain't shittin' around do it 'fore somebody comes along and gets a glimpse of eem. I cain't have all this stirrin' around right now. I got a blanket in back of my car. I'll go get it and we'll wrap eem in that. You have him down from there by the time I walk back, hear me?"

Boots turned and looked at the tree and didn't say anything.

"Hear me talkin' to ya Boots, I mean it. Get him down from there," Rube said as he turned and headed down the hill towards his car.

Boots was standing with black oily soot smeared on the front of his shirt looking down at the body that lay on the ground at his feet. He was still out of breath and coughing deep hacking coughs when Rube walked back over the hill and handed him a corner of the blanket and they laid it out next to the corpse. Rube stood behind and pushed and tilted the body with his foot and it rolled on to its side then tipped and rocked back atop his boot.

"Come over here and help me. I ain't got no gloves with me and I don't wanna touch it," Rube said.

Boots stepped over beside Rube and they both pushed until the carcass rolled stiffly over on to the edge of the blanket. Rube knelt down and pulled the blanket over the body and rolled it into a neat tube. They could hear the rattle of the truck as they walked back toward the road, each one dragging a corner of the blanket up the hill and across the grassy pasture.

# STRAY

IT HAD BEEN ALMOST TWELVE whole days before they found the burnt corpse. It smelled so bad when they cut it down that Daddy and Boots had to hold handkerchiefs over their faces. They still gagged and heaved like they were gonna be sick. It was covered in an old wool blanket when they took it out of the back of the truck. By the time they pulled in, a small crowd had started to gather. When Bo Stevens went to step down from the bed of the truck he got so nervous from everybody watching him that he lost his balance and bobbled down on to his knee and an arm dropped out from under the blanket and dangled for a minute before he could steady himself and push it back under. They said it didn't even look like an arm. It looked more like a burnt pecan branch. Daddy said it must have been a real slow burn because it damn near burned him plumb up. Bones and all. Burned all of the skin off and burned its ears off, the fire got so hot it even melted the eyes right out of its head. You could still see the rope where it had soldered to his neck. You couldn't even really tell that it was a human being. Just looked like charcoal. Black and chalky and all ashed over. That's what Daddy said anyway. Elgie asked if we could look at it and Daddy said that we had better not. He said he even had a hard time looking. Things like that never seemed to bother Daddy much, so I figured it must have been real bad. The body stayed down there for the longest time until the smell just got too bad to take. Nobody ever came up and claimed it. Daddy came out and said that he was gonna get to the bottom of it but when nobody reported any coloreds to be missing he just went on to doing something else. The blacks must have been too scared to come out and say that they were missing some kin or else it was just a stray that just happened in to the wrong place at the wrong time. People talked about it for a while until the trucks started rolling in. Trucks with dog houses full of pickers just spilling over the sides. After that all that seemed to be on people's minds was cotton. Even the coloreds lost interest in talking about it. It seemed strange to me how everything just went on like it always had. Once people got to picking and thinking about their crop that's usually how things went. Nobody seemed to be too concerned with anything else. I guess they were all just too tired to think about anything else.

We were all glad to see Esther the day she came walking up in the yard. She walked into the house and straight into the kitchen and started rattling around like she hadn't missed a beat. She gave me a hug when I told her that I was sorry about PV. She hugged me tight for a long time and I thought she might cry but she didn't. She just said, 'thank you', and told me that I was a good and kind young'n. Elgie walked in and started to sit down and then he turned and gave her a little hug too and told her that it was nice to see her. Daddy ate that morning like he hadn't eaten in a week. I guess none of us really had eaten in a long time. Just pushed the food around on the plate with our forks. A couple of times the women's league from over at the Baptist church had brought food over but I think they were trying to impress Daddy because they brought real fancy things that weren't fit to eat. Some of them brought over pies and we ate those mostly.

## ALL HOPE

THE FRONT AXLE BOWED and the right wheel tilted inward. An inch wide space is all that kept the rubber from rubbing against the fender as she wrenched on the steering wheel and turned into town. The engine chugged and sputtered under the downshift, and the car jerked around the corner and hopped into the reflective gauntlet of store fronts that lined the street. She watched as the surreal image of herself drifted in the hypnotic churn of the engine, her gaunt face and sunken eyes staring back at her, desperate and yearning. An old woman sat crooked and slouching barelegged and barefoot on the seat beside her in a dirty green dress and sucked deep heavy drags off of her cigarette, holding the thick smoke down in her lungs before expelling it with hacking coughs into the cab. The putrid hag sat up and hacked violently several times and then leaned her face over and spit thick, yellow mucous out the window on to the street then sat back and drew the smoke again down deep into her lungs. Three children, half clothed, bounced around the back seat. The smallest of the three lunged forward and hung over the seat and wrapped his arms around Maggie's neck and pulled her head to his face. She took one hand from the wheel and fanned back behind her head swatting him in his face and shooing him like a fly. He bounced back on to the seat and sat crying between the others who just ignored him and continued to wrestle around.

Maggie felt the pounding in her temples as the sobbing and fussing rang out behind her, and the coughing and hacking and spitting filled the air with the stench of slow stale rot. She kept her eyes fixed on the road in front of her and gripped the wheel so tight in her hands until they turned cold and white as milk. She loosened them letting the blood rush back in before gripping and wrenching the wheel again. She could see in the mirror as her possessions rattled in the wind behind her. The rope wrapped tight around them, slack blowing and slapping against the rear fender.

Rube watched from the window as the car turned into the curb and came to a stop. He could see Maggie sitting behind the wheel. He watched as she stepped from the car, her dress wadded and dingy in the sunlight. Faces turning downward as she stepped through the door and made her way to his office.

"Hey Rubal, you busy?" she asked, standing in the doorway.

"Hey there Maggie, come on in. I ain't that busy I don't reckon."

He motioned her to the chair in front of his desk.

"Naw, thanks anyway. I don't need to sit down I ain't gonna stay. Mama and the babies is sittin' out there in the heat. I just come by to talk to you a minute."

She took a little white cloth and patted her face and around her eyes.

"It sure is hot, don't you think?"

Rube could tell that she did not want him to know how badly she was trying to hide her tears but he knew anyway.

"Hotter than it's been in a while I'd say."

He knew why she was here and he didn't feel the need to make her ask the question she had come here to ask.

"Ya know Maggie, I went out and looked for Guppy, but I gotta tell ya I don't have no idea where he might've gotten off to. I cain't find anybody who remembers the last time they even saw eem. A lot of 'em say they've seen eem but they just cain't remember when or even where."

"Rubal, do you think he just run off from me or do you think somethin' mighta happened to eem?"

"Maggie to tell you the truth, I just don't have no idea. I s'pect he mighta had somethin' to do with that mess we found out yonder. He's been spoutin' off about such nonsense for a while and I think he mighta just done more than talk this time. I s'pose if anything's happened to eem we'd find out sooner or later but as much as I hate to say it I'd bet that he did just run off and we're libel to never find eem. 'Less he wants to be found that is."

Maggie walked over and sat down and patted the cloth on her face again.

"Maggie, I know it don't seem like it right now, but I'm tellin' ya you're better off if we don't find eem. Matter of fact we'd all be better off if he just stays wherever he is. He ain't nothin' but trouble Maggie, that's all he's ever been."

"I know."

"I see that your car is packed up. Ya'll goin on a trip somewheres?"

"Yeah sort of. Mama's got family over in Oklahoma City. A cousin anyway. Her husband runs some kinda store over there and they said I might could work there some."

"Well, now that sounds like it might be real good. Might work out nice for ya."

"Yeah, I don't know. I just know I got to get away from here is all. Ain't nothin' for me here now. I done give up on this damned ol' town," she looked at Rube and tried to smile.

"Thanks Rubal. You always been nice to me."

"Well now, you don't give up all hope. I'm gonna keep askin' around and maybe Guppy'll turn up and if he does I'll get word to ya. You write me when you get settled in up there and let me know how things are goin' and where I can get a hold of ya."

Maggie didn't say anything else as she stood and walked to the door. She turned and smiled again as she walked out and slid back in behind the steering wheel. The car jumped and sputtered to life and backed away from the curb and rolled to the end of the street and headed east.

About a week later Daddy got a call. Seems just this side of Oklahoma City Maggie turned her car and drove straight off into the Canadian River. State Police said she never even touched her brakes. That car flew forty feet into that river and sank right to the bottom. Drowned herself, her mama and all three of them kids.

Daddy seemed sullen and just a little sad for several days after he got that call.

## PRECIOUS METAL

RUBE PULLED THE CAR ONTO THE shoulder and eased it over until the tires rested on the edge of the ditch. He sat for a long time staring out across the pasture toward the hill and the spindly branches that peeked up over the crest, still leafless and lifeless and black. He had driven this same road nearly every day of his life. He had sat stiffening his neck and keeping his eyes fixed straight ahead into the dust as the soft grass swayed and rolled across the field and the branches squiggled up against the sky, beckoning him to look like the snake laden head of Medusa. He had sung chorus' of 'I'll Fly Away' over and over in his mind as the rantings and ravings of his father poured out around him and hung above the growl of the engine, buzzing down at him relentless as a thousand flies. He felt the knot in the pit of his stomach when he had walked over the hill and seen Boots standing in the shadow of his past. He wanted to run. He wanted to run back over that hill and just keep on running. As far away from there as he could. So far and fast that he might even be able to outrun himself.

The truck passed by so close that it shook his car and he jumped and fanned the dust as it swirled behind and drifted in around him. The arm of the driver extended out the window and waved as the truck vanished in the slinging gravel that peppered the front of the sedan.

"Slow that damn thing down," Rube said to himself as he pushed open the door and stepped out on to the road.

He walked around the front of the car, inspected the hood and licked his finger and rubbed at a small chip near the grill.

"Crazy fool," he said, slinging his hand at the empty road in the direction that the truck had gone.

He stood for a minute, then walked back to the car, opened the door and sat back down and reached to turn the key.

"Aw hell," he said as he stood back up and walked around the car and stepped into the ditch.

Rube stomped his feet heavy in the tall grass and high-stepped over to the fence and mashed the wire with his foot and stepped over into the field. He climbed to the top of the hill and looked down at the tree. He felt the old familiar knot kneading at his insides as he shuffled down the slope.

A dark shadow seeped up the trunk and spiraled around the outstretched limb where the black soot had drifted from the flame and painted the tree. He walked beneath the limb and put his hands behind his back and closed his eyes. He tried to imagine the men that had stood in that exact spot. He had often wondered what had gone through their minds as they waited for the rope to tighten and hoist them from the ground and stretch the life out of them. Robbing their wives and children of fathers and husbands. He stepped from beneath the tree, walked a short distance and turned back to face it. Time had not dulled the sharp and cutting images that still flashed vivid in his mind. He could still taste the smell of kerosene that drifted from the flames and hung in his throat, and he could see the colors of black and orange and white flashing in front of him. The laughter and screaming and pounding still echoed in his ears, and in the stillness around him it rang out so loudly that it drowned out the soft cooing of the doves that sat high in the branches and called back and forth above him.

The crude plank cross still leaned propped against the tree trunk charred from the heat, and he could feel the tears as they rolled down his cheeks and dripped off his chin. He took the handkerchief from his back pocket and squatted down on his haunches and wiped at his eyes. He thought of PV laying out there stretched across the belly of his mule. The sharp twinge of shame that shot through his gut was dulled by the shadow of the charred cottonwood and the realization that such a sudden, uneventful death was a merciful compromise to the evils that he had seen men do to other men beneath its branches.

The sun sank just enough to let its silvery white rays slide beneath the limb and into the dry, powdery dust below. A golden gleam flashed and then was snuffed out and then flashed again as a thin cloud floated past.

"What the hell?"

He stood and wiped his eyes again and stuffed the cloth back into his pocket and inched his way to the spot that had produced the flash.

With the toe of his boot he stirred the ground and the sifted dust produced a small gold, black and chalky clump. He knelt and picked it up and raised it to his mouth and blew the dirt from its surface. He pulled the handkerchief back out and rubbed at the black soot until the dull ore began to shine with the lustre of precious metal. The gold had melted and run together, and as he rubbed he saw the left half of the old pointed Mason insignia. He stood pondering the melted, gold ring and leaned back against the tree trunk and stared up at the charred limb.

"Well I'll be damned. Guppy Walters?"

Rube stepped over to the cross and tilted it forward and examined its front and back and then laid it on the ground and pulled it apart and leaned the two planks back against the tree.

He stood staring at the melted ring and then at the limb for several minutes.

"Guppy Walters. I will be damned."

The sun beginning to burn itself out as it continued to fall. He stood on the hill and turned back to look at the tree and wiped at his eyes as he crossed the pasture and pulled away, sending dust and gravel swirling into the air behind him.

## SLEEPING DOGS

"SAY BOOTS," RUBE SAID AS HE stepped through the door.

Boots was scribbling and concentrating hard on a form that he was trying to fill out.

"Hey there, Rube. Whatcha know?"

"What'd they do with that burnt niggra? I mean where'd they take it? Did they say?"

"You know I didn't even think to ask where they were gonna take it. I s'pose they buried it don't you? Why? What'd you want with it anyway?"

"Oh nothin' in particular, I just wanted to see somethin', that's all."

"Well I guess I can find out for ya, if you want me to."

"Naw it ain't no big deal. I was just wantin' to see somethin' but it ain't no big deal."

"Oh by the way, I saw Sonny and his gang out wanderin' around. Ya know they ain't headed for nothin' but trouble I tell you that right now. Anyway they said they saw Guppy a while back drunk and layin in the grass hollerin' about nigger this and nigger that and how he's gonna finish some job or some nonsense. He just ain't gonna let it go is he. He's just gonna keep stirrin' it around 'til we got a whole bed of fire ants down here too ain't he. I swear I'd like to," Boots clinched his fist and gritted his teeth at Rube.

"Aw he ain't gonna get nobody stirred up. Things been too quiet for too long. People ain't gonna wanna get into all that mess again. Things been nice and quiet here for too long. 'Sides he might just have decided to go somewhere where things were a bit more rowdy. Lord I hope so. Ya know, just don't be doin' no more askin' around 'bout all this. You know how everybody gets around here when they get to talkin' about somethin' or another. I don't wanna put any more ideas into the few idiots minds that are runnin' wild around here. I mean, you saw that thing. Hell Boots, who could do somethin' like that to another human being. Damnedest thing I ever seen. Let's just let it lie. I mean people already thinkin' about other things. They don't need us comin' along pokin' at the ant bed. The way that body was burned damn near plumb up, we ain't never gonna know who it was for sure. I mean let's just let sleepin' dogs lie."

"Well, hell, Rube you's the one..."

"I know, I know I was." Rube interrupted. "But I been thinkin' about it and hell it just ain't worth stirrin' it all up that's all. At the end of the day we still gonna have just what we got right now. A few crazies that for the most part keep quiet, and a sorryass, drunk trouble maker who ain't around causin' us no more trouble. Hell he might come back if he gets wind that we're lookin' for eem. I don't know about you but I'll trade that crazy old sonuvabitch for one burnt up niggra vagrant any old day. No matter how bad it is, if that's what it takes to get ridda the likes of him then so be it."

"You think he had somethin' to do with it?" Boots said.

"Hell yes I do, Boots. I know damn well he did. Don't you?"

"Aw, hell yes. Don't know who mighta helped eem, but hell yes I think he had somethin' to do with it."

"Well I don't know who mighta helped eem either. Don't know anybody else that twisted. Hell he prob'ly got drunk and did it by hisself."

"Yeah maybe you right. Maybe. Either way I'm like you, glad to be rid of eem."

Rube walked into his office and shut the door. He sat down behind his desk and took out the distorted clump of gold and laid it out in front of him.

"Guppy Walters. I will be damned."

## PLANKS

JACK ROUNDED THE CORNER and watched as the sedan pulled up in the yard and stopped just shy of the grass. He snorted and stomped his feet as the door popped open. He laid his ears back and neighed out at the house and looked to see if Esther had heard him but she did not appear on the front porch like she had done before. He bellowed again as he walked to the far side of the pen away from the man who was walking toward him.

"Ho there," Rube said to the anxious mule as he stepped into the pen.

He stood in the pen for a moment then crossed the yard to the house. He looked out across the yard to the east and again to the west and then stepped up on to the porch.

Several sizes of odd shaped and colored cans sat scattered atop darkened spots that seeped out beneath them where the water had soaked into the rough wood. Little green sprigs stuck up from the dark, moist soil and draped over the rims of the cans, their ends busting open in bright bursts of color exploding in sharp contrast against the various shades of gray that covered the porch and the house. He sat down in the rocking chair, took his hat off, wiped at his forehead and looked across the yard at the pen and the field that lay stretched out behind it. He could see the tan, powdery folds where the rock and matted sand had been pried up and loosened from the earth in scraped rows that stretched across from one side to the other and he watched as Jack walked into the lean-to and passed like a shadow behind the opening of the two missing planks.

"Well I will be damned."

## MAMA

DADDY GOT A CALL AT HOME one night and they said that Sonny and those other boys that he ran around with got drunk and stole a car. Apparently Sonny got into a fight with one of the other boys and hit him in the head with a tire iron that was laying on the back floor board. I guess all the other boys were scared for themselves because they turned on him and said that they tried to get him to stop but he was like a maniac hitting that boy in the head. He really only hit him in the head one time and he told Daddy that it was more an accident than anything else. A week later that boy died. Daddy said that was too much trouble for him to do anything about and Sonny finally had to face up to his own actions. He got ten years in the state penitentiary down at Huntsville. I don't really know what that had to do with Mama. I guess Daddy had just gotten tired of trying to help people that he didn't feel like were trying to help themselves. It was shortly after that when he decided that he had indeed done all he could do for Mama. I remember the morning that he took her away like it was yesterday.

The thump and drag and thump and drag started at the top of the stairs and continued until they were at the bottom. He gently leaned her back, balancing her against the wall. He turned away and then turned back again, touching her on the shoulder and reassuring himself that she was indeed balanced and that she would not slide down the wall in either direction, then turned back to the stairs. He took the stairs in a hop clearing three steps at a time until he was back at the top. A small leather bag and two hard-shell cases embossed on the sides with the artificial print of some exotic skin sat atop the landing and he grabbed them and skipped back down to the bottom. She stood with her eyes glassy and fixed in a vacant stare as if looking through an invisible window into some other world. He took her arm and laced it in with his and turned her toward the door. She followed beside him as he stepped out on to the porch. Her eyes still wide and fixed, undaunted by the bright light of the afternoon sun.

Esther was standing in the hall that day when he led Mama out. Me and Elgie were out on the front porch. I wanted to run off and hide but Daddy said that we should be there to see her off, even if she didn't know that we were there at all. She looked so white in the sun. Gray like the color of a ghost. I hadn't noticed the dark pits beneath her eyes but in the sun they stuck out bad from beneath her bonnet. She was a stranger to me standing there on the porch. Some kind of unrelated tenant who had been living in the upstairs room. Daddy took her hand and led her toward the car and she never even turned back to look at us or the house or anything. She just slid on to the seat and stared out the windshield. Elgie walked off around the side of house, but I stood there and watched them drive away. I stood there and watched until that big sedan wasn't nothing but a tiny little fleck of pepper down in the road. I spent the rest of the day like Elgie, feeling sorry for myself. When Esther got ready to leave that night, Daddy drove her home. That was the first time he had done that. I went into our room and pulled off my clothes for bed. It had been a day that I was more than anxious to put as far behind me as I could. When I went to put my things up on the dresser there it was. That yellow and black handle. Hand carved bone. Not cheap and brittle like those butter and molasses handles on them two-bit Barlows that filled the bucket next to the cash register.

KIN

DON'T REALLY KNOW HOW come me to give that knife to Arliss. They's just sumpin' 'bout seein them two little ol' boys standin' there watchin' they mama taken off like that. It was 'bout all I could do but to feel sorry for 'em. Seems funny how they almost startin' to feel like kin to me. 'Sides that boy been eyein' that knife ever since he first laid eyes on it. Ain't no Uncle Henry neither. Whatever that is. Oh my daddy give it to me alright, but just 'cause he got hisself a new one. Said he gonna throw it away and don't care if I have it or not. I cain't help but laugh thinkin' 'bout that boy's eyes fixed on it big around as two saucers. Boy startin' to feel just like kin to me.

# DAMNEDEST THING

YELLOW THICK AND WARM seeped from the prick wound and ran out over the white rubbery mass and diluted itself in the clear greasy liquid that pooled on the plate. Rube pinched a piece of biscuit and mopped it all around the edge, sopped up the yolk and dropped it in his mouth and licked at his fingers.

"Well I guess they not ever gonna print a story on that burnt niggra," Rube said as he thumbed through the paper.

"I ain't never seen nobody burnt up like that though, I tell ya. Lookin' back at it, I don't s'pose they never gonna find out who it was, I mean I couldn't really even tell you if he was a black man or a white man. Ain't that funny. Everybody makes such a fuss over black and white and let somebody burn up like that and you cain't even tell the difference. Ain't that the damnedest thing, Esther? Huh. Esther, I got to tell you, you sure got a talent when it comes to these biscuits. Pure talent that's what it is," Rube said as he finished the last bite and headed out the door.

The gravel popped and crackled beneath the rubber as the tires rolled out the drive. He pulled and pushed the rear view mirror until it held the faint picture of the two of them standing on the front porch, wiggly and jumping in the vibration that emanated up from the engine block through the dash and the windshield and into the metal frame of the mirror. Elgie stood with his arm draped over the shoulder of his little brother. Rube smiled to himself when Arliss raised his hand and waved as they watched him pull away. He could see in the open window above them the lace curtains that drifted, blowing in and out of the room that he used to call his, and he knew that things would never be the way they once had been. Down the side of the house toward the back, Esther stood amidst the damp, clean sheets and hung them across the wire line and pinned them to dry in the breeze. He watched them blur in the distance as he made his way down the road toward town, passing the grassy ravines that lined the road. The fences of wood and wire that marked the boundaries of the pastures and fields flourishing in the thick heat that hung above them. He rolled down his window and hung his elbow out and breathed deep as the countryside flashed by around him. He could feel the lump of gold in his shirt pocket and he took it out and held it in his hand. He knew the right thing to do, and he knew that his wife was never going to really be a wife to him again, much less a mother to those boys. She'd probably stay right where she was as far as he knew. They were good boys. Growing up better than he ever thought they would. The way they had dealt with everything. Esther was good for them. Good for him too. He needed the help. Coming in from town and cooking and cleaning and doing the work of a woman was almost too much for him to think about. Besides, things had finally started to feel like they might be alright. Like him and the boys might just be able to get along. The thought of farming for a living passed across his mind as he glanced out the window at the overgrown acres that stretched out around the house, the little clump of gold flashing back at him as he drove. He wasn't real sure of too many things anymore, but the one thing he was sure of was that whatever had happened to Orville Walters he had brought on himself and as far as he could see, Guppy deserved whatever he got. He thought about PV and his mules. Just a man trying to get by. That's all. Trying to scratch something out of this world just like everybody else. He knew damn good and well that Guppy and a few of the others would have never stopped until something bad happened to PV.

And why? Just because they had been brought up that way. Born and bred mean. He had seen that kind of meanness before. So simple and pure that it was just downright evil. It seemed to travel in the veins and filter out purer and purer as it passed through the generations. It came from some ancient time and had survived like a plague to be passed on from one to another with no real understanding of where it had originated or even a thought as to how it might ever be remedied. He hated it. He didn't really give a damn about what color a man was. Not really. Least not enough to want to hurt one because of it. He didn't really give a damn about that mule either. And why would anybody else give a damn about it? Nothing about that whole situation had changed one thing around here except for the fact that it just bothered people. Just bothered them because they didn't have anything better to be bothered about. Just a rundown black man out there driving a rundown team across land that wasn't fit for nothing. Never had been as far back as he could remember. PV never had bothered anybody as far as he knew. He felt ashamed at times that he wasn't strong enough to stand up and say that. He had even thought at times that if PV had been a white man he was pretty sure that they would have been friends. He could still hear the endless rantings of his father. He had laid in his bed and listened and watched him pacing in the hall and flailing his arms and yelling (out that rancid, ignorant word over and over at the top of his lungs) nigger, nigger, nigger. And for no apparent reason. No black man had ever done a thing to his father. Not one thing. He had not wanted to, but he had overheard and overseen the men standing outside talking and scheming. His father climbing into the truck throwing the strange gestures and secret handshakes, hooded and psychotic beneath the white robe. He had prayed many times to be delivered from that world. He cried hard on the day that his father had died. But unlike the tears of other children at the graves of their fathers, he cried tears of relief. Tears held inside behind false valiancy that poured out in a deluge like the tears of soldiers who manage to return home mangled in body and spirit, but alive. He had sworn to himself that he would not allow any such vice to fester and enslave him the way hatred had snared his father.

"Aw hell," he said as he hung his arm back out the window and slung his hand as hard as he could out at the overgrown ravine. The little clump of gold flashed in the sun as it flew out across the road and bounced off into the tall grass.

A chalky caliche cloud curled and rose up like a dry white wave and flooded the ditch and the grass and the air as it followed the shiny black sedan up the road.

## FIGURED IT FOR COLORED

I KNEW ALL ALONG THAT Daddy had poisoned Rosie. The night before he took Mama away I heard him in her room talking to her. She wasn't listening but he was talking all the same. Told her about Guppy and how they never even really looked at the body when they brought it in. On account of it was so burnt up and nasty looking and they just figured it for colored anyhow. I guess it was all just too much for him to carry around and he had to tell somebody. I saw the shame in his eyes and I tried for a long time to hate him for it, but after all, who'd've ever thought somebody'd get that upset over an old mule dyin'.

# ABOUT THE AUTHOR

Stacy Dean Campbell is a novelist whose work explores memory, race, and moral reckoning in the American South and Southwest. His fiction is known for its spare, lyrical prose and unflinching emotional honesty. He lives in Tennessee.